George S. Hillard, M. François Guizot

Essay on the Character and Influence of Washington

in the Revolution of the United States of America

George S. Hillard, M. François Guizot

Essay on the Character and Influence of Washington
in the Revolution of the United States of America

ISBN/EAN: 9783337230548

Printed in Europe, USA, Canada, Australia, Japan

Cover: Foto ©Andreas Hilbeck / pixelio.de

More available books at **www.hansebooks.com**

ESSAY

ON THE

CHARACTER AND INFLUENCE

OF

WASHINGTON

IN THE

REVOLUTION OF THE UNITED STATES OF AMERICA.

BY M. GUIZOT.

TRANSLATED FROM THE FRENCH.

THIRD EDITION.

NEW YORK:

PUBLISHED BY JAMES MILLER,

(SUCCESSOR TO C. S. FRANCIS & CO.,)

522 BROADWAY.

1868.

TRANSLATOR'S PREFACE.

THE following Essay is a translation of the Introduction, by M. Guizot, to a French version of Sparks's Life of Washington, and of selected portions of Washington's Writings, which has recently appeared in Paris, in six octavo volumes. M. Guizot is well known, not only as the author of many valuable historical works, but as a practical statesman himself, and therefore peculiarly qualified to appreciate the character of Washington, and to estimate his claims to the gratitude of his country, and the admiration of mankind. The Essay can hardly fail to be read with interest by every countryman of the illustrious man who forms its subject. It is a performance remarkable for the knowledge which it evinces of our own history, for its great political wisdom, its elevated moral tone, and its just discrimination in regard to the character of Washington. Every American citizen must be highly gratified to find his own veneration for the name of Washington confirmed by this unbiassed tribute from a foreigner so distinguished in literature and politics, as M. Guizot. Nothing has ever been written concerning him in Europe, so accurate, so just, and so profound as this; and it will serve to justify and strengthen that admiration, which has been accorded to him in foreign countries, hardly less than in his own.

GEORGE S. HILLARD.

ADVERTISEMENT

OF THE FRENCH PUBLISHERS.

No foreign event occurring at a distance ever awakened so lively a sympathy in France, as the Revolution of the United States of America. No great man who was a foreigner has ever, in this country, been the object of general admiration to such an extent as Washington. He has had the applause of both the court and the people, of the old *régime* and the new nation. During his life, testimonials of respect were heaped upon him by Louis the Sixteenth; and, at his death, Napoleon directed a public mourning for him, and a funeral oration.*

* "Bonaparte rendered unusual honors to the name of Washington, not long after the event of his death was made known in France. By what motives he was prompted, it is needless to inquire. At any rate, both the act itself and his manner of performing it are somewhat remarkable, when regarded in connexion with his subsequent career. He was then First Consul. On the 9th of February, he issued the following order of the day to the army. "Washington is dead! This great man fought against tyranny; he estab

It is now forty years since this great man has been reposing, to use his own expression, " in the mansions of rest," at Mount Vernon, by the side of his fathers. But his country has recently reared to him the noblest of monuments, in the publication of his *Works*, consisting of his Letters, Discourses, and Messages, comprising what was written and spoken by him in the midst of his active career, and forming indeed his lively image and the true history of his life.

These are, in truth, his *Works*. Washington preserved with scrupulous care, either a first draft or an exact copy of every letter he wrote, whether as a public man or a private individual,

lished the liberty of his country. His memory will always be dear to the French people, as it will be to all free men of the two worlds ; and especially to French soldiers, who like him and the American soldiers, have combated for liberty and equality. The First Consul likewise ordered, that during ten days, black crape should be suspended from all the standards and flags throughout the Republic. On the same day a splendid ceremony took place in the Champ de Mars, and the trophies brought by the army from Egypt were displayed with great pomp. Immediately after this ceremony was over, a funeral oration, in honor of Washington (*Éloge Funèbre de Washington*) was pronounced by M. de Fontanes, in the Hôtel des Invalides, then called the Temple of Mars. The First Consul, and all the civil and military authorities of the capital, were present."—Sparks's *Life of Washington*, pp. 531, 532, *note*.

and whether they related to his own concerns, the management and culture of his farms, or to the interests of the state. During the period from 1783 to 1787, in his retirement at Mount Vernon, he arranged the first part of this correspondence, containing among other things, whatever had been written by him during the war of independence ; and, at his death, he bequeathed all his papers, together with his estate at Mount Vernon, to his nephew, Bushrod Washington, who was for thirty years one of the justices of the Supreme Court of the United States. The entire collection, comprising the letters written by Washington himself, and those addressed to him, filled more than two hundred folio volumes.

The Congress of the United States has recently purchased these precious papers, and caused them to be deposited in the national archives. An able editor, Mr. Sparks, already well known by his important historical labors, and especially by editing the " Diplomatic Correspondence of the United States during the War of Independence," (printed at Boston in twelve octavo volumes), has examined these papers and made selections and extracts from them. The family of Washington, his surviving friends, and various intelligent and distinguished persons favored his efforts in executing this patriotic task. Mr. Sparks has not remained content with the collection of materials, already so ample, which was in his possession; he traveled over America and Europe, and the public and private collections of France and England were liberally opened to him. He has sought out, and brought together from all quarters, the documents necessary to illustrate and complete this authentic biography of a great man, which is the history of the infant years of a great people ; and a work in twelve large octavo volumes, adorned with portraits, plates, and *fac-similes*, under the title of " The Writings of George Washington," has been the result of this labor, which has been performed in all its parts with scrupulous fidelity, patriotism, and a love of the subject.

The work is divided into several parts.

The First Volume contains a Life of Washington, written by Mr. Sparks.

The Second Volume, entitled Part First, contains the Official and Private Letters of Washington, prior to the American Revolution, (from the 9th of March, 1754, to the 31st of May, 1775). The official letters relate to the war of 1754–1758, between France and England, for the possession of the territories lying west of the English colonies.

The Third, Fourth, Fifth, Sixth, Seventh, and Eighth Volumes (being the Second Part) comprise the Correspondence and the various papers relating to the American Revolution and the War of Independence, (from the 16th of June, 1775, to the 23d of December, 1783).

The Ninth Volume (being the Third Part) is composed of the Private Letters written by Washington from the end of 1783 to the spring of 1789, in the interval between his return to Mount Vernon, after the peace of Versailles, and his elevation to the Presidency of the United States, (from the 28th of December, 1783, to the 14th of April, 1789).

The Tenth and Eleventh Volumes (being the Fourth Part) comprise the Official and Private Correspondence of Washington from his elevation to the Presidency to the close of his life, (from the 5th of May, 1789, to the 12th of December, 1799).

The Twelfth Volume (being the Fifth Part), contains the Documents and Messages addressed by Washington to Congress, as President of the United States, and also his Proclamations and Addresses to the American people in general, or to particular classes of citizens.

Each volume is terminated by an Appendix, in which the Editor has collected a variety of his-

torical documents of great interest, and, generally
speaking, hitherto unpublished, which illustrate
the principal events of the period, and the most
important parts of the life and character of
Washington.

Finally, numerous and accurate Notes, scattered through the work, give all the information
necessary for the complete understanding of the
letters and incidents to which they relate.

Viewed as a whole and in its details, in its
literary execution and in its outward form, the
edition is worthy of the great name to which it
is consecrated.

In 1838, when the work had been just com-
pleted, the American Editor, desirous that Washington should be as well known in France as in
his own country, applied to M. Guizot, requesting him to make a selection, from the voluminous
correspondence, of such portions as seemed most
calculated to awaken an interest in the French
public, and to superintend their publication in
the French language. M. Guizot has made this
selection; upon the principle of taking, especially, First, the letters concerning the relations of
France and the United States at that period, and
the distinguished part which our country acted
in that great event; Secondly, those which develope the political views of Washington in the

formation of the constitution and the organization of the government of the United States,—
views full of valuable instruction ; Thirdly, those
which exhibit in the clearest light the character,
the turn of mind, and the manners of the great
man from whom they proceeded.

In order to accomplish fully the honorable task
which he undertook, M. Guizot was desirous of
presenting his own views of the character of
Washington, and of his influence in the revolution which founded the United States of
America ; and these are contained in the Introduction, which is prefixed to our edition.

We have spared no pains to make its ex-
ternal appearance worthy of the intrinsic value
of its contents.   We are indebted to the kindness of General Cass, the minister of the United
States in France, for most useful assistance and
information ; and he has afforded them with a
kindness, at once so enlightened and so gener-
ous, that we feel it our duty to make a public
acknowledgment of our obligations to him.

CHARACTER AND INFLUENCE

OF

WASHINGTON.

———— ◆•◆•◆ ————

Two difficult and important duties are
assigned to man, and may constitute his
true glory; to support misfortune and resign himself to it with firmness; to believe
in goodness and trust himself to it with
unbroken confidence.

There is a spectacle not less noble or
less improving, than that of a virtuous man
struggling with adversity; it is that of a
virtuous man at the head of a good cause,
and giving assurance of its triumph.

If there were ever a just cause, and one
which deserved success, it was that of the
English colonies in their struggle to become the United States of America. In
their case, open insurrection had been pre-

ceded by resistance. This resistance was founded upon historical right and upon facts, upon natural right and upon opinions.

It is the honorable distinction of England to have given to her colonies, in their infancy, the seminal principle of their liberty. Almost all of them, either at the time of their being planted or shortly after, received charters which conferred upon the colonists the rights of the mother country. And these charters were not a mere deceptive form, a dead letter, for they either established or recognized those powerful institutions, which impelled the colonists to defend their liberties and to control power by dividing it; such as the laying of taxes by vote, the election of the principal public bodies, trial by jury, and the right to meet and deliberate upon affairs of general interest.

Thus the history of these colonies is nothing else than the practical and sedulous development of the spirit of liberty, expanding under the protecting influence of the laws and traditions of the country. Such, indeed, was the history of England itself.

A still more striking resemblance is presented in the fact, that the colonies of America, at least the greater part of them and the most considerable among them, either were founded, or received their principal increase, precisely at the period when England was preparing to sustain, or was already sustaining, those bold conflicts against the claims of absolute power, which were to confer upon her the honorable distinction of giving to the world the first example of a great nation, free and well governed.

From 1578 to 1704, under Elizabeth, James the First, Charles the First, the Long Parliament, Cromwell, Charles the Second, James the Second, William the Third, and Queen Anne, the charters of Virginia, of Massachusetts, of Maryland, of Carolina, and of New York, were, one after another, recognized, contested, restrained, enlarged, lost, regained; incessantly exposed to those struggles and those vicissitudes, which are the condition, indeed the very essence, of liberty; for it is victory, and not peace, that free communities can lay claim to.

At the same time with their legal rights, the colonists had also religious faith. It was not only as Englishmen, but as Christians, that they wished to be free; and their faith was more dear to them than their charters. Indeed, these charters were, in their eyes, nothing more than a manifestation and an image, however imperfect, of the great law of God, the Gospel. Their rights would not have been lost, even had they been deprived of their charters. In their enthusiastic state of mind, supported by divine favor, they would have traced these rights to a source superior and inaccessible to all human power; for they cherished sentiments more elevated than even the institutions themselves, over which they were so sensitively watchful.

It is well known, that, in the eighteenth century, the human understanding, impelled by the accumulation of wealth, the growth of population, and the increase of every form of social power, as well as by its own impetuous and self-derived activity, attempted the conquest of the world. Political science, in all its forms, woke into new and vigorous life; as did, to a still greater degree, the spirit of philosophy, proud, unsatisfied, eager to penetrate and to regulate all things. English America shared in this great movement, but serenely and dispassionately; obeying its inherent tendency rather than rushing into new and untried paths. Philosophical opinions were there combined with religious belief, the triumphs of reason with the heritage of faith, and the rights of man with those of the Christian.

A noble spectacle is presented to us, when we see the union of historical and rational right, of traditions and opinions. A nation, in such a case, gains in prudence as well as in energy. When time-honored and esteemed truths control man without enslaving him, restrain at the same time that they support him, he can move onward and upward, without danger of being carried away by the impetuous flight of his own spirit, soon to be either dashed in pieces against unknown obstacles, or to sink gradually into a sluggish and paralyzing inactivity. And when, by a further union, still more beautiful and more salutary, religious belief is indissolubly linked,

2

in the very mind of man, to the general progress of opinions, and liberty of reason to the firm convictions of faith,—it is then that a people may trust themselves to the boldest institutions. For religious belief promotes, to an incalculable extent, the wise management of human affairs. In order to discharge properly the duty assigned to him in this life, man must contemplate it from a higher point of view; if his mind be merely on the same level with the task he is performing, he will soon fall below it, and become incapable of accomplishing it in a worthy manner.

Such was the fortunate condition, both of man and of society, in the English colonies, when, in a spirit of haughty aggression, England undertook to control their fortunes and their destiny, without their own consent. This aggression was not unprecedented, nor altogether arbitrary; it also rested upon historical foundations, and might claim to be supported by some right.

It is the great problem of political science, to bring the various powers of society into harmony, by assigning to each its sphere and its degree of activity; a har-

mony never assured, and always liable to
be disturbed, but which, nevertheless, can
be produced, even from the elements of the
struggle itself, to that degree which the
public safety imperatively demands. It is
not the privilege of states in their infancy
to accomplish this result. Not that any
essential power is in them absolutely disre-
garded and annihilated; on the contrary,
all powers are found in full activity; but
they manifest themselves in a confused
manner, each one in its own behalf, without
necessary connexion or any just proportion,
and in a way to bring on, not the struggle
which leads to harmony, but the disorder
which renders war inevitable.

In the infancy of the English colonies,
three different powers are found, side by
side with their liberties, and consecrated by
the same charters,—the crown, the proprie-
tary founders, whether companies or individuals, and the mother country. The
crown, by virtue of the monarchical principle, and with its traditions, derived from
the Church and the Empire. The proprie-
tary founders, to whom the territory had
been granted, by virtue of the feudal prin-

ciple, which attaches a considerable portion of sovereignty to the proprietorship of the soil. The mother country, by virtue of the colonial principle, which, at all periods and among all nations, by a natural connexion between facts and opinions, has given to the mother country a great influence over the population proceeding from its bosom.

From the very commencement, as well in the course of events as in the charters, there was great confusion among these various powers, by turns exalted or depressed, united or divided, sometimes protecting, one against another, the colonists and their franchises, and sometimes assailing them in concert. In the course of these confused changes, all sorts of pretexts were assumed, and facts of all kinds cited, in justification and support either of their acts or their pretensions.

In the middle of the seventeenth century, when the monarchical principle was overthrown in England in the person of Charles the First, one might be led to suppose, for a moment, that the colonies would take advantage of this to free themselves entirely from its control. In point of fact, some of them, Massachusetts especially, settled by stern Puritans, showed themselves disposed, if not to break every tie which bound them to the mother country, at least to govern themselves, alone, and by their own laws. But the Long Parliament, by force of the colonial principle, and in virtue of the rights of the crown which it inherited, maintained, with moderation, the supremacy of Great Britain. Cromwell, succeeding to the power of the Long Parliament, exercised it in a more striking manner, and, by a judicious and resolute principle of protection, prevented or repressed, in the colonies, both royalist and Puritan, every faint aspiration for independence.

This was to him an easy task. The colonies, at this period, were feeble and divided. Virginia, in 1640, did not contain more than three or four thousand inhabitants, and in 1660 hardly thirty thousand.* Maryland had at most only twelve thousand. In these two provinces the royalist party had the ascendency, and greeted

* Marshall's *Life of Washington,* edition of 1805, Vol. I. p. 76. Bancroft's *History of the United States,* Vol. I. pp. 210, 232, 265.

with joy the Restoration. In Massachusetts, on the other hand, the general feeling was republican; the fugitive regicides, Goffe and Whalley, found there favor and protection; and when the local government were compelled to proclaim Charles the Second as king, they forbade, at the same time, all tumultuous assemblies, all kinds of merry-making, and even the drinking of the King's health. There was, at that time, neither the moral unity, nor the physical strength, necessary to the foundation of a state.

After 1688, when England was finally in possession of a free government, the colonies felt but slightly its advantages. The charters, which Charles the Second and James the Second had either taken away or impaired, were but imperfectly and partially restored to them. The same confusion prevailed, the same struggles arose between the different powers. The greater part of the governors, coming from Europe, temporarily invested with the prerogatives and pretensions of royalty, displayed them with more arrogance than power, in an administration, generally speaking, inconsistent, irritating, seldom successful, frequently marked by grasping selfishness, and a postponement of the interests of the public to petty personal quarrels.

Moreover, it was henceforth not the crown alone, but the crown and the mother country united, with which the colonies had to deal. Their real sovereign was no longer the king, but the king and the people of Great Britain, represented and mingled together in Parliament. And the Parliament regarded the colonies with nearly the same eyes, and held, in respect to them, nearly the same language, as had lately been used towards the Parliament itself, by those kings whom it afterwards overcame. An aristocratic senate is the most intractable of masters. Every member of it possesses the supreme power, and no one is responsible for its exercise.

In the mean time, the colonies were rapidly increasing in population, in wealth, in strength internally, and in importance externally. Instead of a few obscure establishments, solely occupied with their own affairs, and hardly able to sustain their own existence, a people was now forming

itself, whose agriculture, commerce, enterprising spirit, and relative position to other
states, were giving them a place and consideration among men.   The mother country, unable to govern them well, had neither
the leisure nor the ill will to oppress them
absolutely.   She vexed and annoyed them
without checking their growth.

And the minds of men were expanded,
and their hearts elevated, with the growing
fortunes of the country.   By an admirable
law of Providence, there is a mysterious
connexion between the general condition of
a country, and the state of feeling among
the citizens; a certain, though not obvious,
bond of union, which connects their growth
and their destinies, and which makes the
farmer in his fields, the merchant in his
counting-room, even the mechanic in his
workshop, grow more confident and high-
spirited, in proportion as the society, in
whose bosom they dwell, is enlarged and
strengthened.   As early as 1692, the General Court of Massachusetts passed a resolution, " that no tax should be levied upon
his Majesty's subjects in the colonies, without the consent of the Governor and Coun-

cil, and the representatives in General Court assembled."* In 1704, the legislative assembly of New York made a similar declaration.† The government of Great Britain repelled them, sometimes by its silence, and sometimes by its measures, which were always a little indirect and reserved. The colonists were often silent in their turn, and did not insist upon carrying out their principles to their extreme consequences. But the principles themselves were spreading among the colonial society, at the same time that the resources were increasing, which were destined, at a future day to be devoted to their service, and to insure their triumph.

Thus, when that day arrived, when George the Third and his Parliament, rather in a spirit of pride, and to prevent the loss of absolute power by long disuse, than to derive any advantage from its exercise, undertook to tax the colonies without their consent, a powerful, numerous, and enthusiastic party,—the national party,—imme-

* Story's *Commentaries on the Constitution,* Vol. I. p. 62.
† Marshall's *Life of Washington,* Vol. II. p. 17.

diately sprang into being, ready to resist, in the name of right and of national honor.

It was indeed a question of right and of honor, and not of interest or physical well-being. The taxes were light, and imposed no burden upon the colonists. But they belonged to that class of men who feel most keenly the wrongs which affect the mind alone, and who can find no repose while honor is unsatisfied. "For, Sir, what is it we are contending against? Is it against paying the duty of three pence per pound on tea, because burdensome? No; it is the right only, that we have all along disputed."* Such was, at the commencement of the quarrel, the language of Washington himself, and such was the public sentiment—a sentiment founded in sound policy, as well as moral sense, and manifesting as much judgment as virtue.

An instructive spectacle is presented to our contemplation, in the number of public associations, which at that time were formed in the colonies ;—associations, local

* Washington to Bryan Fairfax. *Washington's Writings,* Vol. II. p. 392.

or general, accidental or permanent; chambers of burgesses and of representatives, conventions, committees, and congresses. Men of very different characters and dispositions there met together; some, full of respect and attachment to the mother country, others, ardently devoted to that American country which was growing up under their eyes and by the labor of their own hands; the former, anxious and dejected, the latter, confident and enthusiastic, but all moved and united by the same elevated sentiment, and the same resolution to resist; giving the freest utterance to their various views and opinions, without its producing any deep or permanent division; on the contrary, respecting in each other the rights of freedom, discussing together the great question of the country with that conscientious purpose, that spirit of justice and discretion, which gave them assurance of success, and diminished the cost of its purchase. In June 1775, the first Congress, assembled at Philadelphia, took measures for the publication of a solemn declaration, for the purpose of justifying the taking up of arms. Two members, one from Virginia,

and one from Pennsylvania, were a part of
the committee charged with the duty of
drawing it up. " I prepared," relates Mr.
Jefferson himself, " a draft of the declaration committed to us. It was too strong for
Mr. Dickinson. He still retained the hope
of reconciliation with the mother country,
and was unwilling it should be lessened
by offensive statements. He was so honest
a man, and so able a one, that he was
greatly indulged, even by those who could
not feel his scruples. We therefore requested him to take the paper, and put it
into a form he could approve. He did so:
preparing an entire new statement, and
preserving of the former only the last four
paragraphs, and half of the preceding one.
We approved and reported it to Congress,
who accepted it. Congress gave a signal
proof of their indulgence to Mr. Dickinson,
and of their great desire not to go too fast
for any respectable part of our body, in
permitting him to draw their second peti-
tion to the King according to his own ideas,
and passing it with scarcely an amendment.
The disgust against its humility was general; and Mr. Dickinson's delight at its

passage was the only circumstance that reconciled them to it. The vote being passed, although further observation on it was out of order, he could not refrain from rising and expressing his satisfaction, and concluded by saying, ' There is but one word, Mr. President, in the paper, which I disapprove, and that is the word *Congress;*' on which Benjamin Harrison rose and said, ' There is but one word in the paper, Mr. President, of which I approve, and that is the word *Congress.*'"*

Such a unanimity of feeling in the midst of so much liberty was not a short-lived wisdom, the happy influence of the first burst of enthusiasm. During the period of nearly ten years, which the great contest occupied, men the most unlike, who were ranked under the banners of the same national party, young and old, enthusiastic and calm, continued to act thus in concert, one portion being sufficiently wise, and the other sufficiently firm, to prevent a rupture. And when, forty-six years afterwards,†

* Jefferson's *Memoirs*, Vol. I. pp. 9, 10.
† Mr. Jefferson wrote his *Memoirs* in 1821.

after having taken part in the violent struggle between the parties which American liberty gave birth to, himself the head of the victorious party, Mr. Jefferson called up anew the recollections of his youth, we may be sure, that it was not without mingled emotions of pain and pleasure, that he recurred to these noble examples of moderation and justice.

Insurrection, resistance to established authority, and the enterprise of forming a new government, are matters of grave importance to men like these, to all men of sense and virtue. Those who have the most forecast, never calculate its whole extent. The boldest would shudder in their hearts, could they foresee all the dangers of the undertaking. Independence was not the premeditated purpose, not even the wish, of the colonies. A few bold and sagacious spirits either saw that it would come, or expressed their desire for it, after the period of resistance under the forms of law had passed. But the American people did not aspire to it, and did not urge their leaders to make claim to it. "'For all what you Americans say of your loyalty,' observed the illustrious Lord Camden, at that time Mr. Pratt, ' I know you will one day throw off your dependence upon this country; and, notwithstanding your boasted affection to it, will set up for independence.' Franklin answered, ' No such idea is entertained in the minds of the Americans; and no such idea will ever enter their heads, unless you grossly abuse them.' ' Very true,' replied Mr. Pratt, 'that is one of the main causes I see will happen, and will produce the event.' '' *

Lord Camden was right in his conjectures. English America was grossly abused; and yet, in 1774, and even in 1775, hardly a year before the declaration of independence, and when it was becoming inevitable, Washington and Jefferson thus wrote; "Although you are taught, I say, to believe, that the people of Massachusetts are rebellious, setting up for independency, and what not, give me leave, my good friend, to tell you, that you are abused, grossly abused. . . . .

I can announce it as a fact, that it is not

---

* Washington's Writings, Vol. II. p. 496.

the wish or interest of that government, or any other upon this continent, separately or collectively, to set up for independence; but this you may, at the same time, rely on, that none of them will ever submit to the loss of those valuable rights and privileges, which are essential to the happiness of every free state, and without which, life, liberty, and property are rendered totally insecure." *   " Believe me, dear Sir, there is not in the British empire a man, who more cordially loves a union with Great Britain than I do. But, by the God that made me, I will cease to exist, before I will yield to a connexion on such terms as the British Parliament propose, and, in this, I think I speak the sentiments of America. We want neither inducement nor power to declare and assert a separation. It is will alone, which is wanting, and that is growing apace, under the fostering hand of our King." †

George the Third, in point of fact,

* Letter to Robert Mackenzie, 9 October, 1774; Washington's Writings, Vol. II. p. 400.

† Letter to Mr. Randolph, 29th November, 1775; Jefferson's *Memoirs and Correspondence*, Vol. I. p. 153.

pledged to the course he was pursuing, and acting under the influence of passionate obstinacy, animated and sustained his ministers and the Parliament in the struggle. In vain were fresh petitions constantly presented to him, always loyal and respectful without insincerity; in vain was his name commended to the favor and protection of God, in the services of religion, according to usual custom. He paid no attention, either to the prayers which were made to him, or to those which were offered to Heaven in his behalf; and by his order the war continued, without ability, without vigorous and well-combined efforts, but with that hard and haughty obstinacy, which destroys in the heart all affection as well as hope.

Evidently the day had arrived, when power had forfeited its claim to loyal obedience; and when the people were called upon to protect themselves by force, no longer finding in the established order of things either safety or shelter. Such a moment is a fearful one, big with unknown events; one, which no human sagacity can predict, and no human government can control, but which, notwithstanding, does sometimes come, bearing an impress stamped by the hand of God. If the struggle, which begins at such a moment, were one absolutely forbidden; if, at the mysterious point in which it arises, this great social duty did not press even upon the heads of those who deny its existence, the human race, long ago, wholly fallen under the yoke, would have lost all dignity as well as all happiness.

Nor was there wanting another condition, also essential, to the legitimate character of the insurrection of the English colonies. They had a reasonable chance of success.

No vigorous hand, at that time, had the management of public affairs in England. The cabinet of Lord North was not remarkable for talent or generosity of feeling. The only eminent man in the country, Lord Chatham, was in the opposition.

The times of extreme tyranny had gone by. Proscriptions, judicial and military cruelties, a general and systematic laying waste of the country; all those terrible

measures, those atrocious sufferings, which
a little while before in the heart of Europe,
in a cause equally just, had been inflicted
upon the Hollanders, would not have been
tolerated in the eighteenth century, by
the spectators of the American contest,
and, indeed, were never thought of by
those who were the most fiercely engaged
in it. On the contrary, a powerful party
was formed, and eloquent voices were
constantly lifted up, in the British Parliament itself, in support of the colonies and
of their rights. This is the glory and
distinction of a representative government,
that it insures to every cause its champions,
and brings even into the arena of politics
those defences, which were instituted for
the sanctuary of the laws.

Europe, moreover, could not be a passive
spectator of such a struggle. Two great
powers, France and Spain, had serious
losses and recent injuries in America itself,
to avenge upon England. Two powers,
whose greatness was of recent growth,
Russia and Prussia, displayed in favor of
liberal opinions a sympathy which was enlightened, though a little ostentatious, and

showed themselves disposed to seize the
occasion of bringing discredit upon England, or of injuring her, in the name of
liberty itself. A republic, formerly glorious and formidable, still rich and honored,
Holland, could not fail to assist America,
against her ancient rival, with her capital,
and her credit. Finally, among the powers
of an inferior rank, all those whose situation rendered the maritime supremacy of
England odious or injurious to them, could
not but feel in favor of the new state a
good will; timid, perhaps, and without
immediate effect, but still useful and encouraging.

By the rarest good fortune, at that time
every thing united and acted in concert in
favor of the insurgent colonies. Their
cause was just, their strength already
great, and their characters marked by
prudence and morality. Upon their own
soil, laws and manners, old facts and
modern opinions, united in sustaining and
animating them in their purpose. Great
alliances were preparing for them in Europe. Even in the councils of the hostile
mother country, they had powerful sup-

port. Never, in the history of human societies, had any new and contested right received so much favor, and engaged in the strife with so many chances of success.

Still by how many obstacles was this undertaking opposed! What efforts and sacrifices did it cost to the generation which was charged with the duty of accomplishing it! How many times did it appear to be, and indeed really was, on the point of being utterly defeated!

In the country itself, among the people in appearance and sometimes in reality so unanimous, independence, when once declared, soon met numerous and active adversaries. In 1775, hardly had the first guns been fired at Lexington, when, in the midst of the general enthusiasm, a company of Connecticut troops was requisite in New York to sustain the republican party against the Tories or Loyalists, a name which the partisans of the mother country had proudly adopted.* In 1775, New York sent important supplies to the Eng-

* Marshall's *Life of Washington*, Vol. II. p. 187.

lish army under the orders of General
Gage.* In 1776, when General Howe arrived upon the shores of the same province,
a crowd of inhabitants manifested their
joy, renewed the oath of fidelity to the
crown, and took up arms in its behalf.†
The feeling was the same in New Jersey,
and the Loyalist corps, levied in these two
provinces, equalled in numbers the contin-
gents furnished by them to the republican
armies.‡ In the midst of this population,
Washington himself was not in safety; a
conspiracy was formed to deliver him up
to the English, and some members of his
own guard were found to be engaged in
it.§ Maryland and Georgia were divided.
In North and South Carolina, in 1776
and 1779, two Loyalist regiments, one of
fifteen hundred, and the other of seven
hundred men, were formed in a few days.

Against these domestic hostilities, Congress and the local governments used, at
first, extreme moderation; rallying the

* Marshall's *Life of Washington*, Vol. II. p. 229.
† Ibid., Vol. II. p. 381.
‡ Ibid., Vol. III. p. 47.   Spark's *Life of Washington*,
Vol. I. p 261.
§ Marshall's *Life of Washington*, Vol. II. p. 364.

friends of independence without troubling themselves with its opponents; demanding nothing from those who would have refused; everywhere exerting themselves by means of writings, correspondence, associations, and the sending of commissioners into the doubtful counties, to confirm their minds, to remove their scruples, and to demonstrate to them the justice of their cause, and the necessity there was for the steps they had taken. For, generally, the Loyalist party was founded upon sincere and honorable sentiments; fidelity, affection, gratitude, respect for tradition, and a love of established order; and from such sentiments it derived its strength. For some time the government contented itself with watching over this party and keeping it under restraint; in some districts, they even entered into treaty with it, to secure its neutrality. But the course of events, the imminence of the danger, the urgent need of assistance, and the irritation of the passions, soon led to a more rigorous course. Arrests and banishment became frequent. The prisons were filled. Confiscations of property com-

menced. Local committees of public safety disposed of the liberty of their fellow-citizens, on the evidence of general
notoriety. Popular violence, in more than
one instance, was added to the arbitrary
severities of the magistrates. A printer
in New York was devoted to the cause
of the Loyalists; a troop of horsemen,
who had come from Connecticut for that
purpose, broke his presses and carried off
his types.* The spirit of hatred and
vengeance was awakened. In Georgia
and South Carolina, on the western frontier of Connecticut and of Pennsylvania,
the struggle between the two parties was
marked with cruelty. Notwithstanding the
legitimate character of the cause, notwithstanding the virtuous wisdom of its leaders,
the infant republic was experiencing the
horrors of a civil war.

Evils and dangers, still more serious,
were every day springing from the national
party itself. The motives which led to the
insurrection were pure; too pure to consist
for any length of time, among the mass at

* Marshall's *Life of Washington*, Vol. II. p. 240.

least, with the imperfections of humanity.
When the people were appealed to in the
name of rights, to be maintained, and honor
to be saved, the first impulse was a general
one.   But, however great may be the favor
of Providence in such great enterprises, the
toil is severe, success is slow, and the gen-
erality of men soon become exhausted
through weariness or impatience.   The
colonists had not taken up arms to escape
from any atrocious tyranny; they had not,
like their ancestors in fleeing from England,
the first privileges of life to regain, personal
security and religious toleration.   They
were no longer stimulated by any urgent
personal motive; there were no social spoils
to be divided, no old and deep-seated passions to gratify. The contest was prolonged
without creating in thousands of retired families those powerful interests, those coarse
but strong ties, which, in our old and violent
Europe, have so often given to revolutions
their force and their misery.   Every day,
almost every step towards success, on the
contrary, called for new efforts and new
sacrifices.   "I believe, or at least I hope,"
wrote Washington, "that there is public

virtue enough left among us to deny ourselves every thing but the bare necessaries
of life, to accomplish this end."* A sub-
lime hope, one which deserved to be re-
warded as it was, by the triumph of the
cause, but which could not raise to its own
lofty elevation all that population, whose
free and concurring support was the condition, and indeed the only means, of success. Depression, lukewarmness, inactivity,
the desire to escape from labors and expenses, soon became the essential evil, the
pressing danger, against which the leaders
had constantly to struggle. In point of fact,
it was among the leaders, in the front ranks
of the party, that enthusiasm and devotedness were maintained. In other instances
of similar events, the impulse of perseverance and self-sacrifice has come from the
people. In America, it was the independent and enlightened classes, who were
obliged to animate and sustain the people
in the great contest in which they were engaged for their country's sake. In the

* Letter to Bryan Fairfax; *Washington's Writings*, Vol.
II. p. 395.

ranks of civil life, the magistrates, the rich
planters, the leading merchants, and, in
the army, the officers, always showed
themselves the most ardent and the most
firm; from them, example as well as coun-
sel proceeded, and the people at large followed them with difficulty, instead of urg-
ing them on. " Take none for officers but
gentlemen," was the recommendation of
Washington, after the war had lasted three
years.* So fully had he been taught by
experience, that these were everywhere devoted to the cause of independence, and
ready to risk every thing and suffer every
thing to insure its success.

These, too, were the only persons who,
at least on their own account, could sustain the expenses of the war, for the State
made no provision for them. Perhaps no
army ever lived in a more miserable condition than the American army. Almost
constantly inferior in numbers to the enemy;
exposed to a periodical and, in some sort,
legalized desertion; called upon to march,

* In his instructions to Colonel George Baylor, 9th of
January, 1777; *Washington's Writings*, Vol. IV. p. 269.

encamp, and fight, in a country of immense extent, thinly peopled, in parts uncultivated, through vast swamps and savage forests, without magazines of provisions, often without money to purchase them, and without the power to make requisitions of them; obliged, in carrying on war, to treat the inhabitants, and to respect them and their property, as if it had consisted of troops in garrison in a time of peace, this army was exposed to great exigencies, and a prey to unheard-of sufferings. "For some days," writes Washington, in 1777, "there has been little less than a famine in camp. A part of the army have been a week without any kind of flesh, and the rest three or four days. The soldiers are naked and starving." . . . . . " We find gentlemen reprobating the measure of going into winter quarters; as much as if they thought the soldiers were made of stocks or stones, and equally insensible of frost and snow; and, moreover, as if they conceived it easily practicable, for an inferior army, under the disadvantages I have described ours to be, to confine a superior one, in all repects well-appointed and provided for a winter's campaign, within the city of Philadelphia, and to cover from depredation and waste the States of Pennsylvania and Jersey." . . . . .

" I can assure those gentlemen, that it is a much easier and less distressing thing to draw remonstrances in a comfortable room by a good fireside, than to occupy a cold, bleak hill, and sleep under frost and snow, without clothes or blankets. I feel superabundantly for the poor soldiers, and, from my soul, I pity those miseries which it is neither in my power to relieve nor prevent."*

Congress, to whom he applied, could do hardly more than he himself. Without the strength necessary to enforce the execution of its orders; without the power of passing any laws upon the subject of taxes; obliged to point out the necessities of the country, and to solicit the thirteen confederated States to provide for them, in the face of an exhausted people, a ruined commerce, and a depreciated paper currency; this assembly, though firm and prudent,

---

* *Washington's Writings*, Vol. V. pp. 199, 200.

was often able to do nothing more than address new entreaties to the States, and clothe Washington with new powers; instructing him to obtain from the local governments, reinforcements, money, provisions, and every thing requisite to carry on the war.

Washington accepted this difficult trust; and he soon found a new obstacle to surmount, a new danger to remove. No bond of union, no central power, had hitherto united the colonies. Each one having been founded and governed separately, each, on its own account, providing for its own safety, for its public works, for its most trifling as well as most important affairs, they had contracted habits of isolation and almost of rivalship, which the distrustful mother country had taken pains to foster. In their relations to each other, even ambition and the desire of conquest insinuated themselves, as if the States had been foreign to each other; the most powerful ones sometimes attempted to absorb the neighboring establishments, or to deprive them of their authority; and in their most important interest, the defence of their fron-

tiers against the savages, they often followed a selfish course of policy, and mutually abandoned one another.

It was a most arduous task to combine
at once, into one system, elements which
had hitherto been separated, without hold-
ing them together by violence, and, while
leaving them free, to induce them to act in
concert under the guidance of one and the
same power. The feelings of individuals
no less than public institutions, passions as
well as laws, were opposed to this result.
The colonies wanted confidence in each
other. All of them were jealous of the
power of Congress, the new and untried
rival of the local assemblies; they were
still more jealous of the army, which they
regarded as being, at the same time, dangerous to the independence of the States
and to the liberty of the citizens. Upon
this point, new and enlightened opinions
were in unison with popular feeling. The
danger of standing armies, and the necessity, in free countries, of perpetually resisting and diminishing their power, their influence, and the contagion of their morals,
was one of the favorite maxims of the

eighteenth century. Nowhere, perhaps, was this maxim more generally or more warmly received than in the colonies of America. In the bosom of the national party, those who were the most ardent, the most firmly resolved to carry on the contest with vigor and to the end, were also the most sensitive friends of civil liberty; that is to say, these were the men, who looked upon the army, a military spirit, military discipline, with the most hostile and suspicious eye. Thus it happened, that obstacles were met with precisely in that quarter in which it was natural to look for, and to expect to find, the means of success.

And in this army itself, the object of so much distrust, there prevailed the most independent and domocratic spirit. All orders were submitted to discussion. Each company claimed the privilege of acting on its own account and for its own convenience. The troops of the different States were unwilling to obey any other than their own generals; and the soldiers, any other than officers, sometimes directly chosen, and always at least approved, by themselves. And the

day after a defeat which it was necessary
to retrieve, or a victory which was to be
followed up, whole regiments would break
up and go home, it being impossible to prevail upon them to wait even a few days
for the arrival of their successors.

A painful doubt, mingled with apprehen-
sion, arises in the mind at the contemplation of the many and severe sufferings with
which the course of the most just revolution is attended, and of the many and perilous chances to which a revolution, the best
prepared for success, is exposed. But this
doubt is rash and unjust. Man, through
pride, is blind in his confident expectation,
and, through weakness, is no less blind in
his despair. The most just and successful
revolution brings into light the evil, physical and moral, always great, which lies
hidden in every human society. But the
good does not perish in this trial, nor in the
unholy connexion which it is thus led to
form; however imperfect and alloyed, it
preserves its power as well as its rights; if
it be the leading principle in men, it pre-
vails, sooner or later, in events also, and

4

instruments are never wanting to accomplish its victory.

Let the people of the United States for ever hold in respectful and grateful remembrance, the leading men of that generaton which achieved their independence, and founded their government! Franklin, Adams, Hamilton, Jefferson, Madison, Jay, Henry Mason, Greene, Knox, Morris, Pinckney, Clinton, Trumbull, Rutledge; it would be impossible to enumerate them all; for, at the time the contest began, there were in each colony, and in almost every county in each colony, some men already honored by their fellow citizens, already well known in the defence of public liberty, influential by their property, talent, or character; faithful to ancient virtues, yet friendly to modern improvement; sensible to the splendid advantages of civilization, and yet attached to simplicity of manners; high-toned in their feelings, but of modest minds, at the same time ambitious and prudent in their patriotic impulses; men of rare endowments, who expected much from humanity, without presuming too much upon themselves, and who risked for their country far more than they could receive from her, even after her triumph.

It was to these men, aided by God and seconded by the people, that the success of the cause was due. Among them, Washington was the chief.

While yet young, indeed very young, he had become an object of great expectation. Employed as an officer of militia in some expeditions to the western frontier of Virginia against the French and Indians, he had made an equal impression on his superiors and his companions, the English governors and the American people. The former wrote to London to recommend him to the favor of the King.* The latter, assembled in their churches, to invoke the blessing of God upon their arms, listened with enthusiasm to an eloquent preacher, Samuel Davies, who, in praising the courage of the Virginians, exclaimed, "As a remarkable instance of this, I many point out to the public that heroic youth, Colonel Washington, whom I cannot but hope Prov-

* Washington's Writings, Vol. II. p. 97.

idence has hitherto preserved in so signal a manner for some important service to his country."*

It is also related, that fifteen years afterwards, in a journey which Washington made to the West, when on the banks of the Ohio, an old Indian at the head of his tribe requested to see him, and told him that, at the battle of Monongahela, he had several times discharged his rifle at him, and directed his warriors to do the same; but, to their great surprise, their balls had no effect. Convinced that Washington was under the protection of the Great Spirit, he had ceased to fire at him, and had now come to pay his respects to a man who, by the peculiar favor of Heaven, could never die in battle.

Men are fond of thinking that Providence has permitted them to penetrate its secret purposes. The anecdote of the old chief became current in America, and formed the subject of a drama, called *The Indian Prophecy*.†

Never, perhaps, was this vague expecta-

---

* August 17th, 1755. Washington's Writings. Vol. II. p. 89.
† Washington's Writings, Vol. II. p. 475.

tion, this premature confidence in the destiny, I hardly venture to say the predestination, of any individual more natural, than in the case of Washington; for there never was a man who appeared to be, and who really was, from his youth, and in his early actions, more consistent with his future career, and more adapted to the cause, upon which he was destined to bestow success.

He was a planter by inheritance and inclination, and devoted to those agricultural interests, habits, and modes of life, which constituted the chief strength of American society. Fifty years later, Jefferson, in order to justify his confidence in the purely democratic organization of this society, said, "It cannot deceive us as long as we remain virtuous, and I think we shall, as long as agriculture is our principal object."* From the age of twenty years, Washington considered agriculture as his principal employment, making himself well acquainted with the prevalent tone of feeling, and sympathizing with the virtuous and simple habits of his country. Traveling, field-

* *Edinburgh Review*, July, 1830, p. 498.

sports, the survey of distant tracts of land, intercourse, friendly or hostile, with the Indians on the frontier, these formed the amusements of his youth. He was of that bold and hardy temperament, which takes pleasure in those adventures and perils, which, in a vast and wild country, man has to encounter. He had that strength of body, perseverance, and presence of mind, which insure success.

In this respect, at his entrance into life, he felt a slightly presumptuous degree of self-confidence. He writes to Governor Dinwiddie; "For my own part I can answer, that I have a constitution hardy enough to encounter and undergo the most severe trials, and, I flatter myself, resolution to face what any man dares."*

To a spirit like this, war was a more congenial employment than field-sports or traveling. As soon as an opportunity offered, he embraced the employment with that ardor, which, in the early period of life, does not reveal a man's capacity so certainly as his taste. In 1754, it is said,

---

* Washington's Writings, Vol. II. p. 29.

when George the Second was hearing a despatch read, which had been transmitted by the Governor of Virginia, and in which Washington, than a young major, ended the narrative of his first battle with the words, "I heard the bullets whistle, and, believe me, there is something charming in the sound;" the King observed, "He would not say so, if he had been used to hear many." Washington was of the King's opinion; for, when the major of the Virginia militia had become the Commander-in-chief of the United States, some one having asked him if it were true, that he had ever expressed such a sentiment, he replied, "If I said so, it was when I was young."*

But his youthful ardor, which was at the same time serious and calm, had the authority which belongs to a riper age. From the first moment in which he embraced the military profession, he took pleasure, far more than in the excitement of battle, in that noble exercise of the understanding and the will, armed with power in order to accomplish a worthy purpose, that power-

* Washington's Writings, Vol. II. p. 39.

ful combination of human action and good
fortune, which kindles and inspires the
most elevated as well as the most simple
minds. Born in the first rank of colonial
society, trained in the public schools in the
midst of his countrymen, he took his place
naturally at their head; for he was at once
their superior and their equal; formed to
the same habits, skilled in the same ex
ercises; a stranger, like them, to all elegant learning, without any pretensions to
scientific knowledge, claiming nothing for
himself, and exerting only in the public
service that ascendency, which always at-
tends a judicious and penetrating understanding, and a calm and energetic character, in a disinterested position.

In 1754, he was just appearing in society,
and entering upon his military career. It
is a young officer of two-and-twenty, who
commands battalions of militia, and cor-
responds with the representative of the king
of England. In neither of these relations
does he feel any embarrassment. He loves
his associates; he respects the king and the
governor; but neither affection nor respect
alters the independence of his judgment or

of his conduct. By an admirable, instinctive power of action and command, he
sees and apprehends, by what means and
upon what terms success is to be obtained
in the enterprise he has undertaken on behalf of his king and his country. And these
terms he imposes, these means he insists
upon; from the soldiers he exacts all that
can be accomplished by discipline, prompt-
ness, and activity in the service; from the
governor, that he shall discharge his duty
in respect to the pay of the soldiers, the
furnishing of supplies, and the choice of
officers. In every case, whether his words
or opinions are sent up to the superior
to whom he is rendering his account, or
pass down to the subordinates under his
command, they are equally precise, practical, and decided, equally marked by that
authority which truth and necessity bestow
upon the man who appears in their name.
From this moment, Washington is the leading American of his time, the faithful and
conspicuous representative of his country,
the man who will best understand and best
serve her, whether he be called upon to

fight or negotiate for her, to defend or to govern her.

It is not the issue alone which has revealed this. His contemporaries foresaw it. Colonel Fairfax, his first patron, wrote to him, in 1756, " Your good health and fortune are the toast at every table."* In 1759, chosen, for the first time, to the House of Burgesses in Virginia, at the moment when he was taking his seat in the House, the Speaker, Mr. Robinson, presented to him, in warm and animated terms, the thanks of the House for the services which he had rendered to his country. Washington rose to make his acknowledgments for so distinguished an honor; but such was his embarrassment, that he could not speak a single word; he blushed, hesitated, and trembled. The Speaker at once came to his aid, and said, "Sit down, Mr. Washington; your modesty equals your valor, and that surpasses the power of any language that I possess."† Finally, in 1774, on the eve of the great struggle, after the

* Washington's Writings, Vol. II. p. 145.
† Spark's *Life of Washington*, Vol. I. p. 107.

separation of the first Congress held for the purpose of making preparations to meet it, Patrick Henry replied to those that inquired of him, who was the first man in Congress, "If you speak of eloquence, Mr. Rutledge, of South Carolina, is the greatest orator; but, if you speak of solid information and sound judgment, Colonel Washington is unquestionably the greatest man on that floor."*

However, to say nothing of eloquence, Washington had not those brilliant and extraordinary qualities, which strike the imagination of men at the first glance. He did not belong to the class of men of vivid genius, who pant for an opportunity of display, are impelled by great thoughts or great passions, and diffuse around them the wealth of their own natures, before any outward occasion or necessity calls for its employment. Free from all internal restlessness and the promptings and pride of ambition, Washington did not seek opportunities to distinguish himself, and never aspired to the admiration of the world. This spirit

* Spark's *Life of Washington*, Vol. I., p. 107.

so resolute, this heart so lofty, was pro-
foundly calm and modest. Capable of rising
to a level with the highest destiny, he might
have lived in ignorance of his real power
without suffering from it, and have found,
in the cultivation of his estates, a satisfac-
tory employment for those energetic faculties, which were to be proved equal to the
task of commanding armies and founding
a government.

But, when the opportunity presented itself, when the exigence occurred, without
effort on his part, without any surprise on
the part of others, indeed rather, as we
have just seen, in conformity with their
expectations, the prudent planter stood
forth a great man. He had, in a remarkable degree, those two qualities which, in
active life, make men capable of great
things. He could confide strongly in his
own views, and act resolutely in conformity
with them, without fearing to assume the
responsibility.

It is always a weakness of conviction,
that leads to weakness of conduct; for man
derives his motives from his own thoughts,
more than from any other source. From

the moment that the quarrel began, Washington was convinced, that the cause of his country was just, and that success must necessarily follow so just a cause, in a country already so powerful. Nine years were to be spent in war to obtain independence, and ten years in political discussion to form a system of government. Obstacles, reverses, enmities, treachery, mistakes, public indifference, personal antipathies, all these incumbered the progress of Washington, during this long period. But his faith and hope were never shaken for a moment. In the darkest hours, when he was obliged to contend against the sadness which hung upon his own spirits, he says, "I cannot but hope and believe, that the good sense of the people will ultimately get the better of their prejudices. . . . . I do not believe, that Providence has done so much for nothing. . . . . . The great Governor of the universe has led us too long and too far on the road to happiness and glory to forsake us in the midst of it. By folly and improper conduct, proceeding from a variety of causes, we may now and then get bewildered; but I hope and trust, that

there is good sense and virtue enough left
to recover the right path before we shall be
entirely lost."*

And at a later period, when that very
France which had so well sustained him
during the war, brought upon him embarrassments and perils more formidable than
war; when Europe, upheaved from its
foundations, was pressing heavily upon his
thoughts, and perplexing his mind, no less
than America, he still continued to hope
and to trust. "The rapidity of national
revolutions appears no less astonishing
than their magnitude. In what they will
terminate is known only to the Great Ruler
of events; and, confiding in his wisdom
and goodness, we may safely trust the issue
to him, without perplexing ourselves to
seek for that, which is beyond human ken;
only taking care to perform the parts assigned to us, in a way that reason and our
own consciences approve."†

The same strength of conviction, the same
fidelity to his own judgment, which he

---

* Washington's Writings, Vol. IX. pp. 5, 383, 392.
† Ibid., Vol. X. p. 331.

manifested in his estimate of things generally, attended him in his practical management of business. Possessing a mind of admirable freedom, rather in virtue of the soundness of its views, than of its fertility and variety, he never received his opinions at second hand, nor adopted them from any prejudice; but, on every occasion, he formed them himself, by the simple observation or attentive study of facts, unswayed by any bias or prepossession, always acquainting himself personally with the actual truth.

Thus, when he had examined, reflected, and made up his mind, nothing disturbed him; he did not permit himself to be thrown into, and kept in, a state of perpetual doubt and irresolution, either by the opinions of others, or by love of applause, or by fear of opposition. He trusted in God and in himself. "If any power on earth could, or the Great Power above would, erect the standard of infallibility in political opinions, there is no being that inhabits the terrestrial globe, that would resort to it with more eagerness than myself, so long as I remain a servant of the public. But as I have found no better guide hitherto, than upright intentions, and close investigation, I shall adhere to those maxims, while I keep the watch."*

To this strong and independent understanding, he joined a great courage, always ready to act upon conviction, and fearless of consequences. "What I admire in Christopher Columbus," said Turgot, "is, not his having discovered the new world, but his having gone to search for it on the faith of an opinion." Whether the occasion was of great or little moment, whether the consequences were near at hand or remote, Washington, when once convinced never hesitated to move onward upon the faith of his conviction. One would have inferred, from his firm and quiet resolution, that it was natural to him to act with decision, and assume responsibility;—a certain sign of a genius born to command; an admirable power, when united to a conscientious disinterestedness.

On the list of great men, if there be some who have shone with a more dazzling lustre, there are none who have been exposed to a more complete test, in war and in civil gov-

* Washington's Writings, Vol. XI. p. 71.

ernment; resisting the king, in the cause
of liberty, and the people, in the cause of
legitimate authority; commencing a revolution and ending it. From the first moment,
his task was clearly manifest in all its extent
and all its difficulty. To carry on the war, he
had not merely to create an army. To this
work, always so diffiult, the creating power
itself was wanting. The United States had
neither a government nor an army. Congress, a mere phantom, whose unity was
only in name, had neither authority, nor
power, nor courage, and did nothing.
Washington was obliged, from his camp,
not only to make constant solicitations, but
to suggest measures for adoption, to point
out to Congress what course they should
pursue, if they would prevent both themselves and the army from becoming an idle
name. His letters were read while they
were in session, and supplied the subject of
their debates; debates, characterized by inexperience, timidity, and distrust. They
rested satisfied with appearances and pro-
mises. They sent messages to the local
governments. They expressed apprehensions of military power. Washington re-

5

plied respectfully, obeyed, and then insisted;
demonstrated the deceptiveness of appearances, and the necessity of a real force to
give him the substance of the power, of
which he had the name, and to insure to
the army the success which they expected
of it. Brave and intelligent men, devoted
to the cause, were not wanting in this assembly, so little experienced in the art of
government. Some of them went to the
camp, examined for themselves, had interviews with Washington, and brought with
them, on their return, the weight of their
own observations and of his advice. The
assembly gradually grew wiser and bolder,
and gained confidence in themselves and in
their general. They adopted the measures,
and conferred upon him the powers, which
were necessary. He then entered into correspondence and negotiations with local
governments, legislatures, committees, magistrates, and private citizens; placing facts
before their eyes; appealing to their good
sense and their patriotism; availing himself,
for the public service, of his personal friend-
ships; dealing prudently with democratic
scruples and the sensitiveness of vanity;

maintaining his own dignity; speaking as became his high station, but without giving offence, and with persuasive moderation; though wisely heedful of human weakness, being endowed with the power, to an extraordinary degree, of influencing men by honorable sentiments and by truth.

And when he had succeeded, when Congress first, and afterwards the different States, had granted him the necessary means of making an army, his task was not finished; the business of the war had not yet commenced; the army did not exist. Here, too, he was obstructed by a complete inexperience, the same want of unity, the same passion for individual independence, the same conflict between patriotic purposes and disorganizing impulses. Here, too, he was obliged to bring discordant elements into harmony; to keep together those which were constantly ready to separate; to enlighten, to persuade, to induce; to use personal influence; and, without endangering his dignity or his power, to obtain the moral fidelity, the full and free support, both of the officers and soldiers. Then only could Washington act as a general, and turn his attention to the war. Or, rather, it was during the war, in the midst of its scenes, its perils, and its hazards, that he was constantly obliged to recommence, both in the country and the army itself, this work of organization and government.

His military capacity has been called in question. He did not manifest, it is true, those striking displays of it which, in Europe, have given renown to great captains. Operating with a small army over an immense space, great manœuvres and great battles were necessarily unknown to him. But his superiority, acknowledged and declared by his companions, the continuance of the war during nine years, and its final success, are also to be taken as proofs of his merit, and may well justify his reputation. His personal bravery was chivalrous even to rashness, and he more than once abandoned himself to this impulse in a manner painful to contemplate. More than once, the American militia, seized with terror, took to flight, and brave officers sacrificed their lives to infuse courage into their soldiers. In 1776, on a similar occasion, Washington indignantly persisted in re-

maining on the field of battle, exerting himself to arrest the fugitives by his example
and even by his hand. "We made," wrote
General Greene the next day, "a miserable,
disorderly retreat from New York, owing
to the disorderly conduct of the militia.
Fellows's and Parsons's brigades ran away
from about fifty men, and left his Excellency
on the ground within eighty yards of the
enemy, so vexed at the infamous conduct
of the troops, that he sought death rather
than life."[*]

On more than one occasion, also, when
the opportunity appeared favorable, he displayed the boldness of the general as well
as the intrepidity of the man. He has been
called the *American Fabius*, it being said
that the art of avoiding battle, of baffling
the enemy, and of temporizing, was his
talent as well as his taste. In 1775, before
Boston, at the opening of the war, this Fabius wished to bring it to a close by a sudden attack upon the English army, which
he flattered himself he should be able to
destroy. Three successive councils of war,

* Washington's Writings, Vol. IV. p. 94.

forced him to abandon his design, but without shaking his conviction, and he expressed bitter regret at the result.* In 1776, in the State of New York, when the weather was extremely cold, in the midst of a retreat, with troops half disbanded, the greater part of whom were preparing to leave him and return to their own homes, Washington suddenly assumed an offensive position, attacked, one after another, at Trenton and Princeton, the different corps of the English army, and gained two battles in eight hours.

Moreover, he understood what was even a much higher and much more difficult art, than that of making war; he knew how to control and direct it. War was to him only a means, always kept subordinate to the main and final object,—the success of the cause, the independence of the country. When, in 1798, the prospect of a possible war between the United States and France occurred to disturb the repose of Mount Vernon, though already approaching to old age

*Washington's Writings, Vol. III. pp. 82, 127, 259, 287, 290 291, 292, 297.

and fond of his retirement, he thus wrote to Mr. Adams, his successor in the administration of the republic. "It was not difficult for me to perceive that, if we entered into a serious contest with France, the character of the war would differ materially from the last we were engaged in. In the latter, time, caution, and worrying the enemy, until we could be better provided with arms and other means, and had better disciplined troops to carry it on, was the plan for us. But if we should be engaged with the former, they ought to be attacked every step."*

This system of active and aggressive war, which, at the age of sixty-six, he proposed to adopt, was one which, twenty-two years before, in the vigor of life, neither the advice of some of the generals, his friends, nor the slanders of some others, his enemies, nor the complaints of the States which were laid waste by the enemy, nor popular clamor, nor the desire of glory, nor the recommendations of Congress itself, had been able to induce him to follow. "I

* Washington's Writings, Vol. XI. p. 309.

know the unhappy predicament I stand in;
I know that much is expected of me; I
know, that without men, without arms,
without ammunition, without any thing fit
for the accommodation of a soldier, little is
to be done; and, what is mortifying, I
know that I cannot stand justified to the
world without exposing my own weakness,
and injuring the cause, which I am determined not to do. . . . . . My own
situation is so irksome to me at times, that,
if I did not consult the public good more
than my own tranquillity, I should, long
ere this, have put every thing on the cast of
a die."*

He persisted in this course during nine
years. Only when the protracted nature of
the contest and the general indifference
were occasioning a feeling of discourage-
ment, akin to apathy, did he determine to
strike a blow, to encounter some brilliant
hazard, to make the country aware of the
presence of his army, and relieve the people's hearts of some of their apprehensions.
It was thus that, in 1777, he fought the

* Washington's Writings, Vol. III p. 284.

battle of Germantown. And when, in the midst of reverses, endured with heroic patience, he was asked what he should do if the enemy continued to advance, if Philadelphia, for instance, should be taken; he replied, "We will retreat beyond the Susquehanna river, and thence, if necessary, to the Alleghany mountains."*

Besides this patriotic calmness and patience, he displayed the same quality in another form, still more praiseworthy. He saw, without chagrin and ill-humor, the successes of his inferiors in command. Still more, when the public service rendered it advisable, he supplied them largely with the means and opportunity of gaining them. A disinterestedness worthy of all praise, rarely found in the greatest minds; as wise as it was noble, in the midst of the envious tendencies of a democratic society; and which, perhaps, we may be permitted to hope, was in his case attended with a deep and tranquil consciousness of his superiority, and of the glory that would follow him.

* Sparks's *Washington*, Vol. I. p. 221.

When the horizon was dark, when re-
peated checks and a succession of misfor-
tunes seemed to throw a doubt upon the
capacity of the Commander-in-chief, and
gave birth to disorders, intrigues, and hostile insinuations, a powerful voice was
quickly raised in his behalf,—the voice of
the army, which loaded Washington with
testimonials of affectionate respect, and
placed him beyond the reach of complaints
and hostile attacks.

In the winter of 1777 and 1778, while
the army was encamped at Valley Forge,
exposed to the most severe hardships, some
restless and treacherous spirits organized
against Washington a conspiracy of considerable magnitude, which penerated into
the Congress itself. He opposed himself to
it with stern frankness, saying, without reserve and without cautious insincerity, all
he thought of his adversaries, and leaving
his conduct to speak for itself. Such a
course, at such a moment, was putting
much at hazard. But the public respect in
which he was held was so profound, the
friends of Washington, Lord Stirling, Lafayette, Greene, Knox, Patrick Henry,

Henry Laurens, supported him so warmly, the movement of opinion in the army was so decided, that he triumphed almost without defending himself. The principal framer of this conspiracy, an Irishman by the name of Conway, after having sent in his resignation, continued to spread against him the most injurious charges. General Cadwalader resented this conduct; a duel was the consequence; and Conway, severely wounded, and believing himself to be near his death, wrote as follows, to Washington.

"I find myself just able to hold the pen during a few minutes, and take this opportunity of expressing my sincere grief for having done, written, or said any thing disagreeable to your Excellency. My career will soon be over; therefore justice and truth prompt me to declare my last sentiments. You are, in my eyes, the great and good man. May you long enjoy the love, veneration, and esteem of these States, whose liberties you have asserted by your virtues."*

* Washington's Writings, Vol. V. p. 517.

In 1779, the officers of a New Jersey regiment, imperfectly paid, burdened with debts contracted in the service, anxious about their future prospects and those of their families, made an official declaration to the legislature of that State, that they would resign in a body, if they were not better treated. Washington blamed them extremely, and required of them to withdraw their declaration; but they persisted in their course. "It was, and still is, our determination to march with our regiment, and to do the duty of officers, until the legislature should have a reasonable time to appoint others, but no longer. We beg leave to assure your Excellency, that we have the highest sense of your ability and virtues; that executing your orders has ever given us pleasure; that we love the service, and love our country; but when that country gets so lost to virtue and justice, as to forget to support its servants, it then becomes their duty to retire from its service."*

Thus, respect for Washington appeared conspicuously, even in the cabals formed

---

* Marshall's *Life of Washington*, Vol. IV. p. 47.

against him, and was mingled with disobedience itself.

In the state of distress and disorganization into which the American army was perpetually falling, the personal influence of Washington, the affection which was felt for him, the desire of imitating his example, the fear of losing his esteem, or even of giving him pain, deserve to be enumerated among the principal causes, which kept many men, both officers and soldiers, at their posts, kindled anew their zeal, and formed among them that military *esprit de corps*, that friendship of the camp, which is a feeling of great strength, and a fine compensating influence in so rough a profession.

It is a privilege of great men, and often a corrupting one, to inspire affection and devotedness, without feeling them in return. This vice of greatness Washington was exempt from. He loved his associates, his officers, his army. It was not merely from a sense of justice and duty, that he sympathized in their sufferings, and took their interests into his own hands with an indefatigable zeal. He regarded them with a truly tender feeling, marked by compassion for the sufferings he had seen them endure, and by gratitude for the attachment which they had shown to him. And when, in 1783, at the close of the war, at Frances's tavern, in New York, the principal officers, at the moment of their final separation, passed in silence before him, each one pressing his hand as he went by, he was himself moved and agitated, at heart and in his countenance, to a degree that seemed hardly consistent with the firm composure of his spirit.

Nevertheless, he never showed to the army any weakness, or any spirit of unworthy compliance. He never permitted it to be the first object of consideration to itself, and never lost an opportunity to inculcate upon it this truth, that subordination and implicit submission, not only to its country, but to the civil power, was its natural condition, and its first duty.

Upon this subject, he gave it, on three important occasions, the most admirable and the most effective of lessons, that of example. In 1782, he rejected, " with great and painful surprise," * (these are his ex-

* Washington's Writings, Vol. VIII. p. 300.

pressions), the crown and the supreme power, which some discontented officers were offering to him. In 1783, on the eve of the disbanding of the troops, having been informed that the draft of an address was circulating through the army, and that a general meeting was about to be held to deliberate upon the means of obtaining by force, that which Congress, in spite of justice, had refused to grant, he expressed, in the orders of the day, his strong disapprobation of the measure, himself called together another meeting, attended in person, recalled the officers to the consideration of their duty and the public good, and then withdrew, before any discussion took place, wishing to leave to the parties themselves the merit of retracing their steps, which was done promptly and generally.* Finally, in 1784 and 1787, when the officers in their retirement attempted to form among themselves the Society of Cincinnati, in order to preserve some bond of union in their dispersed condition, and for the mutual aid of themselves and their families, as soon as

W..shington's Writings, Vol. VIII. pp. 392-400.

Washington saw that the uneasiness and distrust of a jealous people were awakened by the mere name of a military society, a military order, notwithstanding the personal inclination which he felt towards the institution, he not only caused a change to be made in its statutes, but publicly declined being its president, and ceased to take any part in it.*

By a singular coincidence, about the same time, Gustavus the Third, king of Sweden, forbade the Swedish officers who had served in the French army during the American war, to wear the order of the Cincinnati, "on the ground, that the institution had a republican tendency not suited to his government." †

"If we cannot convince the people that their fears are ill-founded, we should, at least, in a degree yield to them," said Washington, upon this subject.‡ He did not yield, even to the people, when the public interest would have suffered from such a course; but he had too just a sense

---

* Washington's Writings, Vol. IX. pp. 26, 127.

† Ibid., Vol. IX. p. 56.

‡ Ibid., Vol. IX. p. 35.

of the relative importance of things to display the same inflexibility, when merely personal interests or private feelings, however reasonable, were in question.

When the object of the war was obtained, when he had taken leave of his companions in arms, mingled with his affectionate regret, and the joy which he felt in the prospect of repose after victory, another feeling may be perceived in his mind, faint indeed, and perhaps even unknown to himself, and this was, a regret in leaving his military life, that noble profession to which he had devoted his best years with so much distinction. It was a highly congenial employment to Washington, whose genius was methodical, and more firm than inventive; who was just, and full of goodwill to all men, but grave, somewhat cold, born for command rather than struggle; in action, loving order, discipline, and subordination of ranks; and preferring the simple and vigorous exercise of power, in a good cause, to the complicated intrigues and impassioned debates of politics.

"The scene is at last closed. . . . . . On the eve of Christmas, I entered these

6

doors an older man by nine years than when I left them. . . . . . I am just beginning to experience that ease and freedom from public cares, which, however desirable, takes some time to realize. It was not till lately I could get the better of my usual custom of ruminating, as soon as I waked in the morning, on the business of the ensuing day; and of my surprise at finding, after revolving many things in my mind, that I was no longer a public man, nor had any thing to do with public transactions. . . . . . I hope to spend the remainder of my days in cultivating the affections of good men, and in the practice of the domestic virtues. . . . . . The life of a husbandman, of all others, is the most delightful. It is honorable, it is amusing, and, with judicious management, it is profitable. . . . . . I have not only retired from all public employments, but I am retiring within myself, and shall be able to view the solitary walk, and tread the paths of private life, with a heartfelt satisfaction. Envious of none, I am determined to be pleased with all; and this, my dear friend, being the order for my march,

I will move gently down the stream of life,
until I sleep with my fathers."*

Washington, in uttering such language,
was not merely expressing a momentary
feeling, the enjoyment of repose, after long-
protracted toil, and of liberty, after a severe
confinement. The tranquil and active life
of a great landed proprietor; those employments, full of interest and free from anxiety; that domestic authority, seldom disputed, and attended with little responsibility;
that admirable harmony between the intelligence of man and the prolific power of
nature; that sober and simple hospitality;
the high satisfaction which springs from
consideration and good-will obtained without effort,—these were truly suited to his
taste, and were the objects of constant preference to his mind. He would probably
have chosen this very life. He enjoyed it;
and he enjoyed, besides, all that could be
added to it by the public gratitude and his
glory, which were delightful in spite of
their importunate claims upon him.

Always of a serious and practical turn of

mind, he made improvements in the cultivation of his estates, embellished his mansion-house, occupied himself with the local interests of Virginia, traced the outline of that great system of internal navigation from east to west, which was destined, at a future period, to put the United States in possession of one-half the new world, established schools, put his papers in order, carried on an extensive correspondence, and took great pleasure in receiving, under his roof, and at his table, his attached friends. "It is my wish," he wrote to one of them, a few days after his return to Mount Vernon, "that the mutual friendship and esteem, which have been planted and fostered in the tumult of public life, may not wither and die in the serenity of retirement. We should rather amuse the evening hours of life in cultivating the tender plants, and bringing them to perfection before they are transplanted to a happier clime."*

Towards the end of the year 1784, M. de Lafayette came to Mount Vernon. Washing-

* Washington's Writings, Vol. IX. p. 6.

ton felt for him a truly paternal affection, the tenderest, perhaps, of which his life presents any trace. Apart from the services rendered by him, from the personal esteem he inspired, and from the attractiveness of his character, apart even from the enthusiastic devotion which M. de Lafayette testified for him, this elegant and chivalrous young nobleman, who had escaped from the court of Versailles to dedicate his sword and his fortune to the yeomanry of America, was singularly pleasing to the grave American general. It was, as it were, a homage paid by the nobility of the old world to his cause and his person; a sort of connecting tie between him and that French society, which was so brilliant, so intellectual, and so celebrated. In his modest elevation of mind, he was flattered as well as touched by it, and his thoughts rested with an emotion full of complacency upon this young friend, whose life was like that of none other, and who had quitted every thing to serve by his side.

"In the moment of our separation," he wrote to him, "upon the road as I traveled, and every hour since, I have felt all that love, respect, and attachment for you, with which length of years, close connection, and your merits have inspired me. I often asked myself, as our carriages separated, whether that was the last sight I should ever have of you. And though I wished to say No, my fears answered Yes. I called to mind the days of my youth, and found they had long since fled to return no more; that I was now descending the hill I had been fifty-two years climbing, and that, though I was blest with a good constitution, I was of a short-lived family, and might soon expect to be entombed in the mansion of my fathers. These thoughts darkened the shades, and gave a gloom to the picture, and consequently to my prospect of seeing you again. But I will not repine; I have had my day."*

Notwithstanding this sad presentiment, and his sincere taste for repose, his thoughts dwelt constantly upon the condition and affairs of his country. No man can separate himself from the place in which he has once held a distinguished position.

---

* Washington's Writings, Vol. IX. p. 77.

"Retired as I am from the world," he writes in 1786, "I frankly acknowledge I cannot feel myself an unconcerned spectator."* The spectacle deeply affected and disturbed him. The Confederation was falling to pieces. Congress, its sole bond of union, was without power, not even daring to make use of the little that was intrusted to it. The moral weakness of men was added to the political weakness of institutions. The States were falling a prey to their hostilities, to their mutual distrust, to their narrow and selfish views. The treaties, which had sanctioned the national independence, were executed only in an imperfect and a precarious manner. The debts contracted, both in the old and new world, were unpaid. The taxes destined to liquidate them never found their way into the public treasury. Agriculture was languishing; commerce was declining; anarchy was extending. In all parts of the country itself, whether enlightened or ignorant, whether the blame was laid on the government, or the want of government,

* Washington's Writings, Vol. IX. p. 189.

the discontent was general. In Europe, the reputation of the United States was rapidly sinking. It was asked if there would ever be any United States. England encouraged this doubt, looking forward to the hour when she might profit by it.

The sorrow of Washington was extreme, and he was agitated and humbled as if he had been still responsible for the course of events. " What, gracious God!" he wrote, on learning the troubles in Massachusetts, " is man, that there should be such inconsistency and perfidiousness in his conduct? It was but the other day, that we were shedding our blood to obtain the constitutions under which we now live; constitutions of our own choice and making; and now we are unsheathing the sword to overturn them. The thing is so unaccountable, that I hardly know how to realize it, or to persuade myself, that I am not under the illusion of a dream."* " We have probably had too good an opinion of human nature in forming our confederation. Experience has taught us, that men will not

* Washington's Writings, Vol. IX. p. 221.

adopt and carry into execution measures the best calculated for their own good, without the intervention of a coercive power."*
" From the high ground we stood upon, to be so fallen, so lost, is really mortifying."†
" In regretting, which I have often done with the keenest sorrow, the death of our much lamented friend, General Greene, I have accompanied it of late with a query, whether he would not have preferred such an exit to the scenes which, it is more than probable, many of his compatriots may live to bemoan."‡

Nevertheless, the course of events, and the progress of general good sense, were also mingling hope with this patriotic sorrow,— a hope full of anxiety and uneasiness, the only one which the imperfection of human things permits elevated minds to form, but which is sufficient to keep up their courage. Throughout the whole Confederation, the evil was felt and a glimpse was caught of the remedy. The jealousies of the States, local interests, ancient habits, democratic

* Washington's Writings, Vol. IX. p. 187.
† Ibid., Vol. IX. p. 167.
‡ Ibid., Vol. IX. p. 226.

prejudices, were all strongly opposed to the
sacrifices which were requisite in order to
form a government in which the central
power should be stronger and more promi-
nent. Still, the spirit of order and union;
the love of America as their country; regret
at seeing it decline in the esteem of man-,
kind; the disgust created by the petty, in-
terminable, and profitless disturbances of
anarchy; the obvious nature of its evils, the
perception of its dangers; all the just opinions and noble sentiments which filled the
mind of Washington, were gradually extending themselves, gathering additional
stréngth, and preparing the way for a happier future. Four years had hardly elapsed
since the peace, which had sanctioned the
acquisition of independence, when a national
Convention, brought together by a general
spontaneous feeling, assembled at Philadelphia, for the purpose of reforming the federal
government. Commencing its session the
14th day of May, 1787, it made choice of
Washington for its president on the same
day. From the 14th of May to the 17th of
September, it was occupied in forming the
Constitution, which has governed the United

States of America for fifty years; deliberating with closed doors, and under influences the most intelligent and the most pure that ever presided over such a work. On the 30th of April, 1789, at the very moment when the Constituent Assembly was commencing its session at Paris, Washington, having been chosen by a unanimous vote, took an oath, as President of the Republic, to maintain and put in force the new-born Constitution, in the presence of the great functionaries and legislative bodies which had been created by it.

Never did a man ascend to the highest dignity by a more direct path, nor in compliance with a more universal wish, nor with an influence wider and more welcome. He hesitated much. In leaving the command of the army, he had openly announced, and had sincerely promised himself, that he should live in retirement, a stranger to public affairs. To change his plans, to sacrifice his tastes and his repose, for very uncertain success, perhaps to be charged with inconsistency and ambition, this was to him an immense effort. The assembling of Congress was delayed; the election of Washington to the presidency, though known, had not been officially announced to him. "For myself," he wrote to his friend, Gen Knox, "the delay may be compared to a reprieve; for, in confidence I tell you, (with the *world* it would obtain little credit,) that my movements to the chair of government will be accompanied by feelings not unlike those of a culprit, who is going to the place of his execution; so unwilling am I, in the evening of a life nearly consumed in public cares, to quit a peaceful abode for an ocean of difficulties, without that competency of political skill, abilities, and inclination, which are necessary to manage the helm."* The message at length arrived, and he commenced his journey. In his Diary, he writes; "About ten o'clock, I bade adieu to Mount Vernon, to private life, and to domestic felicity; and, with a mind oppressed with more anxious and painful sensations than I have words to express, set out for New York, with the best disposition to render service to my country, in obedience to its call, but

---

* Washington's Writings, Vol. IX. p. 488.

with less hope of answering its expectations."* His journey was a triumphal procession; on the road, and in the towns, the whole population came out to meet him, with shouts of applause and prayers in his behalf. He entered New York, conducted by a committee of Congress, in an elegantly decorated barge, rowed by thirteen pilots, representing the thirteen States, in the midst of an immense crowd in the harbor and upon the shore. His own state of feeling remained the same. "The display of boats," says he in his Diary, "which attended and joined on this occasion, some with vocal and others with instrumental music on board; the decorations of the ships, the roar of cannon, and the loud acclamations of the people, which rent the sky as I passed along the wharves, filled my mind with sensations as painful (contemplating the reverse of this scene, which may be the case, after all my labors to do good,) as they were pleasing."†

About a century and a half before, on the

---

* Washington's Writings, Vol. X. p. 461.
† Marshall's *Life of Washington*, Vol. V. p. 159.

banks of the Thames, a similar crowd and
like outward signs of feeling had attended
Cromwell to Westminster, when he was
proclaimed Protector of the Commonwealth
of England. "What throngs! what acclamations!" said his flatterers. Cromwell
replied, "There would be still more, if
they were going to hang me."

A singular resemblance, and also a noble
difference between the sentiments and the
language of a corrupted great man and a
virtuous great man.

Washington was, with reason, anxious
about the task which he undertook. The
sagacity of a sage, united to the devotedness of a hero, constitutes the highest glory
of humanity. The nation, which he had
conducted to independence, and which required a government at his hands, being
hardly yet formed, was entering upon one
of those social changes which render the
future so uncertain, and power so perilous.

It is a remark often made, and generally
assented to, that in the English colonies,
before their separation from the mother
country, the state of society and feeling was
essentially republican, and that every thing

was prepared for this form of government. But a republican form of government can govern, and, in point of fact, has governed societies essentially different; and the same society may undergo great changes without ceasing to be a republic. All the English colonies showed themselves, nearly in the same degree, in favor of the republican constitution. At the North and at the South, in Virginia and the Carolinas, as well as in Connecticut and Massachusetts, the public will was the same, so far as the form of government was concerned.

Still, (and the remark has been often made,) considered in their social organization, in the condition and relative position of their inhabitants, these colonies were very different.

In the South, especially in Virginia and North Carolina, the soil belonged, in general, to large proprietors, who were surrounded by slaves or by cultivators on a small scale. Entails and the right of primogeniture secured the perpetuity of families. There was an established and endowed church. The civil legislation of England, bearing strongly the impress of its feudal origin, had been maintained almost without exception. The social state was aristocratic./

In the North, especially in Massachusetts, Connecticut, New Hampshire, Rhode Island, &c., the fugitive Puritans had brought with them, and planted there, strict democracy with religious enthusiasm. Here, there was no slavery; there were no large proprietors in the midst of an inferior population, no entailment of landed property; there was no church, with different degrees of rank, and founded in the name of the State; no social superiority, lawfully established and maintained. Man was here left to his own efforts and to divine favor. The spirit of independence and equality, had passed from the church to the state. /

Still, however, even in the northern colonies, and under the sway of Puritan principles, other causes, not sufficiently noticed, qualified this character of the social state, and modified its development. There is a great, a very great difference between a purely religious and a purely political democratic spirit. However ardent, however impracticable the former may be, it receives in its origin, and maintains in its action, a powerful element of subordination and order, that is, reverence. In spite of their spiritual pride, the Puritans, every day, bent before a master, and submitted to him their thoughts, their heart, their life; and on the shores of America, when they had no longer to defend their liberties against human power, when they were governing themselves in the presence of God, the sincerity of their faith and the strictness of their manners, counteracted the inclination of the spirit of democracy towards individual lawlessness and general disorder. Those magistrates, so watched, so constantly changed, had still a strong ground of support, which rendered them firm, often even severe, in the exercise of authority. In the bosom of those families, so jealous of their rights, so opposed to all political display, to all conventional greatness, the paternal authority was strong and much respected. The law sanctioned rather than limited it. Entails and inequality in inheritance were forbidden; but the father had the entire disposition of his property, and divided it among his children according to his own

will. In general, civil legislation was not
controlled by political maxims, and preserved the impress of ancient manners. In
consequence of this, the democratic spirit,
though predominant, was everywhere met
by checks and balances.

Besides, a circumstance of material importance, temporary, but of decisive effect,
served to conceal its presence and retarded
its sway. In the towns, there was no populace; in the country, the population was
settled around the principal planters, com-
monly those who had received grants of the
soil, and were invested with the local mag-
istracies. The social principles were democratic, but the position of individuals was
very little so. Instruments were wanting
to give effect to the principles. Influence
still dwelt with rank. And on the other
hand, the number did not press heavily
enough to make the greater weight in the
balance.

But the Revolution, hastening the progress of events, gave to American society a
general and rapid movement in the direction of democracy. In those States where
the aristocratic principle was still strong, as

in Virginia, it was immediately assailed and subdued. Entails disappeared. The church lost not only its privileges, but its official rank in the State. The elective principle prevailed throughout the whole government. The right of suffrage was greatly extended. Civil legislation, without undergoing a radical change, inclined more and more towards equality.

The progress of democracy was still more marked in events than in laws. In the towns, the population increased rapidly, and with it, the populace also. In the country towards the west, beyond the Alleghany mountains, by a constant and accelerated movement of emigration, new States were growing up or preparing to be formed, inhabited by a scattered population, always in contest with the rude powers of nature and the ferocious passions of savages; half savage themselves; strangers to the forms and proprieties of thickly settled communities; given up to the selfishness of their own separated and solitary existence, and of their passions; bold, proud, rude, and passionate. Thus, in all parts of the country, along the sea-board as well as in the interior of the continent, in the great centres of population, and in the forests hardly yet explored, in the midst of commercial activity and of rural life, numbers, the simple individual, personal independence, primitive equality, all these democratic elements were increasing, extending their influence, and taking, in the State and its institutions, the place which had been prepared for them, but which they had not previously held.

And, in the course of ideas, the same movement, even more rapid, hurried along the minds of men and the progress of opinion, far in advance of events. In the midst of the most civilized and wisest States, the most radical theories obtained not only favor but strength. " The property of the United States has been protected from the confiscation of Britain, by the joint exertions of all, and therefore ought to be the common property of all; and he that attempts opposition to this creed, is an enemy to equity and justice, and ought to be swept from the face of the earth. . . . . . They are determined to annihilate all debts, public and private, and have agrarian laws, which are easily effected by the means of unfunded paper money, which shall be a tender in all cases whatever."* These disorganizing fancies were received in Massachusetts, Connecticut, and New Hampshire, by a considerable portion of the people; twelve or fifteen thousand men took up arms, in order to reduce them to practice. And the evil appeared so serious, that Madison, the most intimate friend of Jefferson, a man whom the democratic party subsequently ranked among its leaders, regarded American society as almost lost, and hardly ventured to entertain any hope.†

Two powers act in concurrence to develope and maintain the life of a people; its civil constitution and its political organization, the general influences of society and the authorities of the State; the latter were wanting to the infant American commonwealth, still more than the former. In this society, so disturbed, so slightly connected, the old government had disappeared, and the new had not yet been formed. I have spoken of the insignificance of Congress,

* Washington's Writings, Vol. IX. p. 207.
† Ibid., Vol. IX. p. 208.

the only bond of union between the States, the only central power; a power without rights and without strength; signing treaties, nominating ambassadors, proclaiming that the public good required certain laws, certain taxes, and a certain army; but not having itself the power of making laws, or judges, or officers to administer them; without taxes, with which to pay its ambassadors, officers, and judges, or troops to enforce the payment of taxes and cause its laws, judges, and officers to be respected. The political state was still more weak and more wavering than the social state.

The Constitution was formed to remedy this evil, to give to the Union a government. It accomplished two great results. The central government became a real one, and was placed in its proper position. The Constitution freed it from the control of the States, gave it a direct action upon the citizens without the intervention of the local authorities, and supplied it with the instruments necessary to give effect to its will; with taxes, judges, officers, and soldiers. In its own interior organization, the central government was well conceived and well balanced; the duties and relations of the several powers were regulated with great good sense, and a clear understanding of the conditions upon which order and political vitality were to be had; at least for a republican form, and the society for which it was intended.

In comparing the Constitution of the United States with the anarchy from which it sprang, we cannot too much admire the wisdom of its framers, and of the generation which selected and sustained them. But the Constitution, though adopted and promulgated, was as yet a mere name. It supplied remedies against the evil, but the evil was still there. The great powers, which it had brought into existence, were confronted with the events which had preceded it and rendered it so necessary, and with the parties which were formed by these events, and were striving to mould society, and the Constitution itself, according to their own views.

At the first glance, the names of these parties excite surprise. Federal and democratic; between these two qualities, these two tendencies, there is no real and essen-

tial difference. In Holland, in the seventeenth century, in Switzerland even in our
time, it was the democratic party which
aimed at strengthening the federal union,
the central government; it was the aristocratic party which placed itself at the head
of the local governments, and defended their
sovereignty. The Dutch people supported
William of Nassau and the Stadtholdership
against John de Witt and the leading citizens of the towns. The patricians of
Schweitz and Uri are the most obstinate
enemies of the federal diet and of its power.

In the course of their struggle, the American parties often received different desig-
nations. The democratic party arrogated
to itself the title of *republican*, and bestowed
on the other, that of *monarchists* and *mono-
crats*. The federalists called their opponents *anti-unionists*. They mutually accused each other of tending, the one to
monarchy, and the other to separation; of
wishing to destroy, the one the republic,
and the other the union.

This was either a bigoted prejudice or a
party trick. Both parties were sincerely
friendly to a republican form of government

and the union of the States. The names, which they gave one another for the sake of mutual disparagement, were still more false than their original denominations were imperfect and improperly opposed to each other.

Practically, and so far as the immediate affairs of the country were concerned, they differed less, than they either said or thought, in their mutual hatred. But, in reality, there was a permanent and essential differ- ence between them in their principles and their tendencies. The federal party was, at the same time, aristocratic, favorable to the preponderance of the higher classes, as well as to the power of the central govern- ment. The democratic party was, also, the local party; desiring at once the rule of the majority, and the almost entire indepen- dence of the State governments. Thus there were points of difference between them, respecting both social order and polit- ical order; the constitution of society itself, as well as of its government. Thus those paramount and eternal questions, which have agitated and will continue to agitate the world, and which are linked to the far higher problem of man's nature and destiny, were all involved in the American parties, and were all concealed under their names.

It was in the midst of this society, so agitated and disturbed, that Washington, without ambition, without any false show, from a sense of duty rather than inclination, and rather trusting in truth than confident of success, undertook actually to found the government which a new-born constitution had just decreed. He rose to his high office, invested with an immense influence, which was acknowledged and received even by his enemies. But he himself has made the profound remark, that "influence is not government."*

In the struggle of the parties, all that had reference to the mere organization of civil society, occupied his attention very little. This involves abstruse and recondite questions, which are clearly revealed only to the meditations of the philosopher, after he has surveyed human societies in all periods and under all their forms. Washington was little accustomed to contemplation, or

* Washington's Writings, Vol. IX. p. 204.

acquainted with science. In 1787, before going to Philadelphia, he had undertaken, for the purpose of getting clear views, to study the constitution of the principal confederations, ancient and modern; and the abstract of this labor, found among his papers, shows, that he had made a collection of facts in support of the plain dictates of his good sense, rather than penetrated into the essential nature of these complicated associations.

Moreover, Washington's natural inclination was rather to a democratic social state, than to any other. Of a mind just, rather than expansive, of a temper wise and calm; full of dignity, but free from all selfish and arrogant pretensions; coveting rather respect than power; the impartiality of democratic principles, and the simplicity of democratic manners, far from offending or annoying him, suited his tastes and satisfied his judgment. He did not trouble himself with inquiring, like the partisans of the aristocratic system, whether more elaborate combinations, a division into ranks, privileges, and artificial barriers, were necessary to the preservation of society. He lived tranquilly in the midst of an equal and sovereign people, finding its authority to be lawful, and submitting to it without effort.

But when the question was one of political and not social order, when the discussion turned upon the organization of the government, he was strongly federal, opposed to local and popular pretensions, and the declared advocate of the unity and force of the central power.

He placed himself under this standard, and did so in order to insure its triumph. But still his elevation was not the victory of a party, and awakened in no one either exultation or regret. In the eyes, not only of the public, but of his enemies, he was not included in any party, and was above them all; "the only man in the United States," said Jefferson, "who possessed the confidence of all; . . . . . . there was no other one, who was considered as any thing more than a party leader."*

It was his constant effort to maintain this honorable privilege. "It is really my wish to have my mind and my actions, which are the result of reflection, as free and inde-

* Jefferson's *Memoirs*, Vol. IV. p. 481.

pendent as the air.* . . . . . . If it should be my inevitable fate to administer the government, I will go to the chair under no preëngagement of any kind or nature whatsoever.† . . . . . Should any thing tending to give me anxiety present itself in this or any other publication, I shall never undertake the painful task of recrimination, nor do I know that I should even enter upon my justification.‡ . . . . . All else is but food for declamation.§ . . . . . Men's minds are as variant as their faces; and, where the motives of their actions are pure, the operation of the former is no more to be imputed to them as a crime, than the appearance of the latter.‖ . . . . . . Differences in political opinions are as unavoidable, as, to a certain point, they may perhap sbe necessary."¶ A stranger also to all personal disputes, to the passions and prejudices of his friends as well as his enemies, the purpose of his whole policy was to maintain this position; and to this policy

---

* Washington's Writings, Vol. IX. p. 84.
† Ibid., Vol. IX. p. 476.   ‡ Ibid., Vol. IX. p. 108.
§ Ibid., Vol. IX. p. 148.
‖ Ibid., Vol. IX. p. 475.   ¶ Ibid., Vol. X. p. 283.

he gave its true name; he called it "the just medium."*

It is much to have the wish to preserve a just medium; but the wish, though accompanied with firmness and ability, is not always enough to secure it. Washington succeeded in this, as much by the natural turn of his mind and character, as by making it his peculiar aim; he was, indeed, really of no party, and his country, in esteeming him so, did no more than pay homage to truth.

A man of experience and a man of action, he had an admirable wisdom, and made no pretension to systematic theories. He took no side beforehand; he made no show of the principles that were to govern him. Thus, there was nothing like a logical harshness in his conduct, no committal of self-love, no struggle of rival talent. When he obtained the victory, his success was not to his adversaries either a stake lost, or a sweeping sentence of condemnation. It was not on the ground of the superiority of his own mind, that he triumphed; but on the ground of the nature of things, and of the

* Washington's Writings, Vol. X. p. 236.

inevitable necessity that accompanied them. Still his success was not an event without a moral character, the simple result of skill, strength, or fortune. Uninfluenced by any theory, he had faith in truth, and adopted it as the guide of his conduct. He did not pursue the victory of one opinion against the partisans of another; neither did he act from interest in the event alone, or merely for success. He did nothing which he did not think to be reasonable and just; so that his conduct, which had no systematic character, that might be humbling to his adversaries, had still a moral character, which commanded respect.

Men had, moreover, the most thorough conviction of his disinterestedness; that great light, to which men so willingly trust their fate; that vast power, which draws after it their hearts, while, at the same time, it gives them confidence that their interests will not be surrendered, either as a sacrifice, or as instruments to selfishness and ambition.

His first act, the formation of his cabinet, was the most striking proof of his impartiality. Four persons were selected by him;

Hamilton and Knox, of the federal party; Jefferson and Randolph, of the democratic. Knox was a soldier, of integrity, of moderate abilities, and easily influenced; Randolph, a restless spirit, of doubtful probity, and little good faith; Jefferson and Hamilton were both sincere, honest, enthusiastic, and able,—the real heads of the two parties.

Hamilton deserves to be ranked among those men, who have best understood the vital principles and essential conditions of government; not merely of a nominal government, but of a government worthy of its mission and of its name. In the Constitution of the United States, there is not an element of order, strength, and durability, to the introduction and adoption of which he did not powerfully contribute. Perhaps he believed the monarchical form preferable to the republican. Perhaps he sometimes had doubts of the success of the experiment attempted in his own country. Perhaps, also, carried away by his vivid imagination and the logical vehemence of his mind, he was sometimes exclusive in his views, and went too far in his inferences. But, of a character as lofty as his mind, he faithfully served the republic, and labored to found and not to weaken it. His superiority consisted in knowing, that, naturally, and by a law inherent in the nature of things, power is above, at the head of society; that government should be constituted according to this law; and that every contrary system or effort brings, sooner or later, trouble and weakness into the society itself. His error consisted in adhering too closely, and with a somewhat arrogant obstinacy, to the precedents of the English constitution, in attributing sometimes in these precedents the same authority to good and to evil, to principles and to the abuse of them, and in not attaching due importance to, and reposing sufficient confidence in, the variety of political forms and the flexibility of human society. There are occasions, in which political genius consists, in not fearing what is new, while what is eternal is respected.

The democratic party, not the turbulent and coarse democracy of antiquity or of the middle ages, but the great modern democracy, never had a more faithful or more distinguished representative than Jefferson. A warm friend of humanity, liberty, and

8

science; trusting in their goodness as well
as their rights; deeply touched by the in-
justice with which the mass of mankind
have been treated, and the sufferings they
endure, and incessantly engaged, with an
admirable disinterestedness, in remedying
them or preventing their recurrence; ac-
cepting power as a dangerous necessity,
almost as one evil opposed to another, and
exerting himself not merely to restrain, but
to lower it; distrusting all display, all personal splendor, as a tendency to usurpation;
of a temper open, kind, indulgent, though
ready to take up prejudices against, and
feel irritated with, the enemies of his party;
of a mind bold, active, ingenious, inquiring,
with more penetration than forecast, but
with too much good sense to push things to
the extreme, and capable of employing,
against a pressing danger or evil, a prudence and firmness which would perhaps
have prevented it, had they been adopted
earlier or more generally.

It was not an easy task to unite these
two men, and make them act in concert in
the same cabinet. The critical state of
affairs at the first adoption of the Constitu-

tion, and the impartial preponderance of Washington alone could accomplish it. He applied himself to it with consummate perseverance and wisdom. At heart, he felt a decided preference for Hamilton and his views. " By some," said he, "he is considered an ambitious man, and therefore a dangerous one. That he is ambitious, I shall readily grant; but it is of that laudable kind, which prompts a man to excel in whatever he takes in hand. He is enterprising, quick in his perceptions, and his judgment intuitively great."* But it was only in 1798, in the freedom of his retirement, that Washington spoke so explicitly. While in office, and between his two secretaries, he maintained towards them a strict reserve, and testified the same confidence in them both. He believed both of them to be sincere and able; both of them necessary to the country and to himself. Jefferson was to him, not only a connecting tie, a means of influence, with the popular party, which was not slow in becoming the opposition ; but he made use of him in the internal administration of his government,

* Washington's Writings, Vol. XI. p. 312.

as a counterpoise to the tendencies, and
especially to the language, sometimes extravagant and inconsiderate, of Hamilton
and his friends. He had interviews and
consultations with each of them separately,
upon the subjects which they were to dis-
cuss together, in order to remove or to
lessen beforehand their differences of opinion. He knew how to turn the merit and
the popularity of each with his own party,
to the general good of the government,
even to their own mutual advantage. He
skillfully availed himself of every opportunity to employ them in a common responsibility. And when a disagreement too
wide, and passions too impetuous, seemed
to threaten an immediate rupture, he inter-
posed, used exhortation and intreaty, and,
by his personal influence, by a frank and
touching appeal to the patriotism and right-
mindedness of the two rivals, he at least
postponed the breaking forth of the evil
which he could not eradicate.

He dealt with things with the same prudence and tact as with men; careful of his
personal position, starting no premature or
superfluous question; free from the restless

desire to regulate every thing and control every thing; leaving the grand bodies of the State, the local governments, and the officers of his administration, to act in their appropriate spheres, and never, except in a case of clear and practical necessity, pledging his own opinion or responsibility. And this policy, so impartial, so cautious, so careful to embarrass neither affairs nor itself, was by no means the policy of an inactive, uncertain, ill-compounded administration, seeking and receiving its opinions and direction from all quarters. On the contrary, there never was a government more determined, more active, more decided in its views, and more effective in its decisions.

It had been formed against anarchy and to strengthen the federal union, the central power. It was entirely faithful to its office. At its very commencement, in the first session of the first Congress, numerous great questions arose; it was necessary to put the Constitution in vigorous action. The relations of the two branches of the Legislature with the President; the mode of communication between the President and the Senate in regard to treaties and the nomination to high offices; the organization of the judiciary; the creation of ministerial departments; all these points were discussed and regulated. A work of vast labor, in which the Constitution was, to some extent, given over a second time to the strife of parties. Without ostentation, without intrigue, without any attempt at encroachment, but provident and firm in the cause of the power which was intrusted to him, Washington, by his personal influence, by an adherence openly given to sound principles, had a powerful influence in causing the work to be carried on in the same spirit which presided over its beginning, and to result in the dignified and firm organization of the government.

His practice corresponded with his principles. Once fairly engaged with public business and parties, this man who, in the formation of his cabinet, showed himself so tolerant, enjoined and observed, in his administration, a strict unity of views and conduct. "I shall not, whilst I have the honor to administer the government, bring a man into any office of consequence knowingly, whose political tenets are adverse to the measures which the general government are pursuing; for this, in my opinion, would be a sort of political suicide."* "In a government as free as ours," he wrote to Gouverneur Morris, at that time residing in London, "where the people are at liberty, and will express their sentiments, (oftentimes imprudently, and, for want of information, sometimes unjustly,) allowances must be made for occasional effervescences; but, after the declaration which I have made of my political creed, you can run no hazard in asserting, that the executive branch of this government never has suffered, nor will suffer, while I preside, any improper conduct of its officers to escape with impunity, nor give its sanction to any disorderly proceedings of its citizens."†

In matters, also, of mere form, and foreign to the usual habits of his life, he was enlightened and directed by a wise tact, a sure instinct as to what is suitable and proper, a regard to which is itself one of the conditions of power. The ceremonials to

* Washington's Writings, Vol. XI. p. 74.
† Washington's Writings, Vol. XI. p. 103.

be observed towards the President became, after his election, a grave party question. Many federalists, passionately attached to the traditions and splendor of monarchy, exulted when at a ball they had succeeded in causing a sofa to be placed on an elevation two steps above the floor of the hall, upon which only Washington and his wife could be seated.* Many of the democrats saw in these displays, and in the public levees of the President, the premeditated return of tyranny, and were indignant, that, receiving at a fixed hour, in his house, all those who presented themselves, he made them only a stiff and slight bow.† Washington smiled at both the delight and the indignation, and persisted in the regulations, surely very modest, which he had adopted. "Were I to give indulgence to my inclinations, every moment that I could withdraw from the fatigue of my station should be spent in retirement. That it is not, proceeds from the sense I entertain of the propriety of giving to every one as free access as consists with that respect which

* Jefferson's *Memoirs*, Vol. IV. p. 457.
† Washington's Writings, Vol. X. p. 99.

is due to the chair of government; and that respect, I conceive, is neither to be acquired nor preserved but by observing a just medium between much state and too great familiarity."*

More serious embarrassments soon put his firmness to a more severe test. After the establishment of the Constitution, the finances formed a question of vast importance to the republic, perhaps the principal one. They were in a state of extreme confusion; there were debts of the Union, contracted at home and abroad; debts of individual States, contracted in their own names, but in behalf of the common cause; warrants for requisitions; contracts for supplies; arrears of interest; also other claims, different in their character and origin, imperfectly known and not liquidated. And at the end of this chaos, there were no settled revenues, sufficient to meet the expenses which it imposed.

Many persons, and, it must be acknowledged, the democratic party in general, were unwilling that light should be thrown into this chaos by assuming all these obli-

, * Washington's Writings, Vol. X. p. 100.

gations, or even by funding them. They would have imposed upon each State its debts, however unequal the burden might have been. They would have made distinctions between the creditors; classifications founded upon the origin of their claims and the real amount of what they had paid for them. In short, all those measures were proposed which, under an appearance of scrupulous investigation and strict justice, were in reality nothing but evasions to escape from or reduce the engagements of the state.

As Secretary of the Treasury, Hamilton proposed the opposite system;—the funding and the entire payment, at the expense of the Union, of all the debts actually contracted for the common benefit, whether with foreigners or Americans, and whoever were the contractors or the present holders, and whatever was the origin of the claims; —the laying of taxes sufficient to secure the redemption of the public debt;—the formation of a national bank, capable of aiding the government in its financial operations, and of sustaining its credit.

This system was the only moral and,

manly one; the only one in conformity with honesty and truth. It strengthened the Union, by uniting the States financially, as they were united politically. It established American credit, by this striking example of fidelity to public engagements, and by the guaranties which it afforded for their fulfilment. It fortified the central government by rallying around it the capitalists, and by giving it powerful means of influence over them and through them.

At the first movement, the opponents of Hamilton did not dare to make any open objection; but they exerted themselves to lessen the authority of the principle, by contesting the equal fairness of the debts, by discussing the honesty of the creditors, and by exclaiming against the taxes. Partisans of local independence, they rejected, instead of viewing with satisfaction, the political consequences of a financial union, and demanded, in virtue of their general principles, that the States should be left, as to the past as well as for the future, to the various chances of their situation and their destiny.

American credit seemed to them to be

bought at too dear a price. They would obtain it, as necessity might require, by means less burdensome and more simple. They found fault with the theories of Hamilton respecting credit, the public debt and its redemption, and banks, as difficult to be understood and fallacious.

But the ultimate effect of the system especially excited their wrath. The aristocracy of wealth is a perilous ally to power; for it is that which inspires the least esteem and the most envy. When the question was on the payment of the public debt, the federal party had on their side the principles of morality and honor. When the public debt, and the speculations founded upon it, were becoming a means of sudden wealth, and perhaps of unlawful influence, the severity of morals passed over to the democratic party, and integrity lent its support to envy.

Hamilton sustained the contest with his usual energy, as pure in his motives as he was firm in his convictions; the head of a party still more than a financier; and, in the administration of the finances, always chiefly occupied with his political object, the foundation of the state, and the strength of its government.

The perplexity of Washington was great. A stranger to financial studies, he had not, upon the intrinsic merit of the proposed questions, a personal conviction derived from knowledge. He felt their justice and their political utility. He had confidence in Hamilton, in his judgment and his virtue. Still, as the debate was prolonged and objections were multiplied, some of them disturbed his mind and others troubled his conscience; and he asked himself with some embarrassment, whether all the reasons were indeed on the side of the government.

I know not which is the more worthy of admiration, the impartiality which inspired these doubts, or the firmness with which, in the final result and after every thing had been well considered, he always sustained Hamilton and his measures. This was a step of great political sagacity. Though it might have been true, that some fallacies were mingled with the financial measures of the Secretary of the Treasury, and some abuses with their execution, a far higher truth predominated in them; by laying the

foundation of the public faith, and by closely connecting the administration of the
finances with the policy of the State, he
gave to the new government, from the first
moment, the consistence of an old and well-
established authority.

The success surpassed the proudest expectations. Confidence appeared in men's
minds, activity in business, and order in
the administration. Agriculture and commerce flourished; credit rose rapidly. Society prospered with a sense of security,
feeling itself free and well-governed. The
country and the government grew strong
together, in that admirable harmony which
is the healthy condition of states.

Washington beheld with his own eyes,
upon every point of the American territory,
this spectacle so glorious and so delightful
to him. In three public journeys, he slowly
traveled over the whole Union, everywhere
received with grateful and affectionate admiration, the only recompense worthy to
affect the heart of a public man. On his
return, he thus wrote; "I am much pleased,
that I have taken this journey. . . . . .
The country appears to be in a very im-

proving state; and industry and frugality are becoming much more fashionable than they have hitherto been. Tranquillity reigns among the people, with that disposition towards the general government, which is likely to preserve it. . . . . . The farmer finds a ready market for his produce, and the merchant calculates with more certainty on his payments. . . . . . Every day's experience of the government of the United States seems to confirm its establishment, and to render it more popular. A ready acquiescence in the laws made under it shows, in a strong light, the confidence, which the people have in their representatives and in the upright views of those who administer the government."*

And almost at the same time, as if Providence had provided that the same testimony should go down to posterity from all parties, Jefferson wrote; " New elections have taken place for the most part, and very few changes made. This is one of many proofs, that the proceedings of the new government have given general satisfaction. . . . . . Our affairs are proceeding in a train of un-

* Washington's Writings, Vol. X. p. 170.

paralleled prosperity. This arises from the
real improvements of our government; from
the unbounded confidence reposed in it by
the people, their zeal to support it, and their
conviction, that a solid union is the best
rock of their safety."*

Thus, when the close of Washington's
presidency approached, when the necessity
of again selecting a chief magistrate for the
nation was near at hand, a general movement was directed towards him, to entreat
him to accept, a second time, the burden of
office. A movement with great diversity,
in spite of its apparent unanimity; the
federal party wished to retain possession of
the power; the democratic opposition felt,
that the time had not come for them to aspire to it, and that the country could not
dispense with the policy, nor with the man,
they nevertheless had a distinct purpose of
attacking. The public were fearful of seeing an interruption of that order and prosperity, so highly valued and so precarious.
But, whether open or concealed, patriotic
or selfish, sincere or hypocritical, the sen-

* Jefferson's *Memoirs*, Vol. III. pp. 93, 112.

timents and opinions of all concurred to the same end.

Washington alone hesitated. His calm and penetrating mind found in his own disinterestedness a freedom, which preserved him from all illusion, both as to affairs and as to himself. The brilliant aspect, the really prosperous condition, of public affairs, did not conceal from his eyes the imminent perils of his situation. From abroad, the intelligence of the French revolution was already startling America. An unavoidable war, commenced with ill success, against the Indians, was requiring considerable efforts. In the cabinet, the disagreement between Hamilton and Jefferson grew very violent; the most urgent intreaties of the President failed to control it; it was almost officially displayed in two newspapers, the *National Gazette* and the *United States Gazette,* fierce enemies under the name of rivals; the known editor of the former was a clerk in Jefferson's department.* Thus encouraged, the opposition press resorted to the most bitter violence, and Washington suffered great uneasiness on account of it.

* His name was Freneau.

9

He wrote to Mr. Randolph, the Attorney-General; "If government, and the officers of it, are to be the constant theme for newspaper abuse, and this too without condescending to investigate the motives or the facts, it will be impossible, I conceive, for any man living to manage the helm or keep the machine together."*

In some parts of the country, especially in Western Pennsylvania, one of the taxes imposed for making provision for the public debt had awakened the spirit of sedition; numerous meetings of the people had declared that they would not pay it; and Washington was compelled to declare in his turn, by an official proclamation, that he would enforce the execution of the laws. In Congress itself, the administration no longer received so constant and powerful a support; Hamilton was, day after day, the object of the most animated attacks; the opposition were unsuccessful in the motions they made against him, but his own plans were not always adopted. Finally, towards Washington himself, the language of the House of Representatives,

* Washington's Writings, Vol. X. p. 287.

always respectful and affectionate, was no longer so full or so tender; on the twenty-second day of February, 1793, the anniversary of his birth, a motion to adjourn the session for half an hour in order to go and pay their respects to him, after being warmly opposed, passed by only a majority of twenty-three votes.

None of these facts, none of these symptoms, escaped the vigilant sagacity of Washington. His natural taste for private life and the repose of Mount Vernon returned with double force. His past success, far from inspiring confidence, made him more fearful for the future. Modestly, but passionately attached to the consideration in which he was held, and to his glory, he was unwilling they should suffer the least abatement. The earnest wish expressed by all would not have been sufficient to determine him; his personal convictions, the public good, the obvious urgency of affairs, the desire or rather the duty of carrying on still further his work yet incomplete, were alone able to overbalance in his mind the dictates of prudence and inclination. He weighed and discussed within himself these different motives, with a more anxious solicitude than seemed to be consistent with his nature, and ended by saying, in the pious weariness of his spirit, " As the all-wise Disposer of events has hitherto watched over my steps, I trust, that, in the important one I may soon be called upon to take, he will mark the course so plainly, as that I cannot mistake the way."*

Unanimously reëlected, he resumed his duties with the same disinterestedness, the same courage, and, in spite of his success, with less confidence, perhaps, than the first time. He had a true presentiment of the trials which awaited him.

There are some events which Providence does not permit those who live at the time of their occurrence to understand; so vast, so complicated, that they far surpass the comprehension of man, and, even when they are exploding, still remain for a long time darkly hidden in the depths, from which proceed those shocks, that ultimately decide the destinies of the world.

Such was the French revolution. Who has measured it? whose judgment and

* Washington's Writings, Vol. X. p. 286.

forecast have not been a thousand times deceived by it, whether friends or foes, admirers or detractors? When the spirit of society and the spirit of man are shaken and convulsed to such a degree, results are produced which no imagination had conceived, no forethought could grasp.

That which experience has taught us, Washington caught sight of from the first day. At the time when the French Revolution had hardly begun, he was already suspending his judgment, and taking his position aloof from all parties and all spectators; free from the presumption of their predictions, from the blindness of their hostility or their hope. " The whole business is so extraordinary in its commencement, so wonderful in its progress, and may be so stupendous in its consequences, that I am almost lost in the contemplation. . . . . . Nobody is more anxious for the happy issue of that business, than I am; as no one can wish more sincerely for the prosperity of the French nation, than I do."* " If it ends as our last accounts, to the first of August, [1789,] predict, that nation will be

* Washington's Writings, Vol. X. p. 89.

the most powerful and happy in Europe; but I fear, though it has gone triumphantly through the first paroxysm, it is not the last it has to encounter before matters are finally settled. . . . . . The mortification of the king, the intrigues of the queen, and the discontent of the princes and no-blesse, will foment divisions, if possible, in the National Assembly; . . . . . the licentiousness of the people on one hand, and sanguinary punishments on the other, will alarm the best disposed friends to the measure. . . . . . To forbear running from one extreme to another is no easy matter; and, should this be the case, rocks and shelves, not visible at present, may wreck the vessel, and give a higher-toned despotism than the one which existed before."* "It is a boundless ocean, whence no land is to be seen."†

From that time, he maintained towards the nations and events of Europe an extreme reserve; faithful to the principles which had founded the independence and the liberties of America, animated by a grateful good-will towards France, and

* Washington's Writings, Vol. X. p. 40.
† Ibid., Vol. X. p. 344.

seizing with earnestness upon every occasion to manifest it, but silent and self-restrained, as if under the presentiment of some grave responsibility of which he should be obliged to sustain the weight, and not wishing to pledge beforehand either his personal opinion or the policy of his country.

When the trying moment arrived, when the declaration of war between France and England caused the great revolutionary struggle to break out in Europe, the resolution of Washington was decided and prompt. He immediately made proclamation of the neutrality of the United States. "My politics are plain and simple; . . . . . to maintain friendly terms with, but be independent of, all the nations of the earth; to share in the broils of none; to fulfil our own engagements; to supply the wants and be carriers for them all; being thoroughly convinced, that it is our policy and interest to do so."* "I want an *American* character, that the powers of Europe may be convinced, we act for *ourselves*, and not for others."† "Regarding

* Washington's Writings, Vol. XI. pp. 382, 102.
† Ibid., Vol. XI. p. 83.

the overthrow of Europe at large as a matter not entirely chimerical, it will be our
prudence to cultivate a spirit of self-depend-
ence, and to endeavor, by unanimity, vigi-
lance, and exertion, under the blessing of
Providence, to hold the scales of our destiny in our own hands.   Standing, as it
were, in the midst of falling empires, it
should be our aim to assume a station and
attitude, which will preserve us from being
overwhelmed in their ruins."*   "Nothing
short of self-respect, and that justice which
is essential to a national character, ought to
involve us in war; for sure I am, if this
country is preserved in tranquillity twenty
years longer, it may bid defiance, in a just
cause, to any power whatever; such, in
that time, will be its population, wealth,
and resources."†

At first, the approbation was general.
The desire for peace, and the reluctance to
express any opinion which might endanger
it, were predominant in men's minds.
Upon the principle of neutrality the cabinet
had been unanimous.   But intelligence

* Washington's Writings, Vol. XI. p 350.
† Ibid., Vol. XI. p. 102.

from Europe was continually arriving, and was spreading like wild-fire through the country. The coalition formed against France assailed the guardian principles of America, the independence and internal liberty of nations. England was at its head, hated as a recent enemy, suspected as a former master. Her decrees and measures in regard to neutral commerce and the impressment of sailors wounded the United States in their dignity and their interests. With the great question of neutrality, particular questions arose, doubtful enough to serve as a just reason or a pretext for diversity of opinions and strong expressions of feeling. Upon some of them, as, for instance, on the restitution of maritime prizes and the mode of receiving the new minister expected from France, the cabinet was no longer unanimous. This minister, M. Genêt, arrived; and his journey from Charleston to Philadelphia was a popular triumph. Everywhere, on his journey, numerous and enthusiastic democratic associations assembled, invited him to meet them, and made addresses to him; the newspapers rapidly circulated through the country accounts of these rejoicings and the news from France. The public feeling grew more and more inflamed. Of an enthusiastic temperament himself, and blindly borne away by the desire of engaging the United States in a war to aid his country, M. Genêt believed himself to have the right and the ability to dare every thing, and to succeed in every thing. He issued letters of marque, enrolled American citizens, armed privateers, adjudged prizes, and acted as a sovereign power in this foreign territory, in the name of republican brotherhood. And when Washington, at first astonished and motionless, but soon determined, vindicated the rights of the general government, Genêt entered into an avowed contest with him, supported his own pretensions, broke out into violent abuse of him, encouraged the spirit of sedition, and even threatened to appeal to the people against a President who was unfaithful to his trust, and to the general cause of liberty.

No head of a state was ever more reserved than Washington in the exercise of power; more cautious in making engagements and taking new steps. But, also, no one ever maintained more firmly his declarations, his purposes, and his rights. He was President of the United States of America. He had, in their name, and by virtue of their constitution, proclaimed their neutrality. The neutrality was to be real and respected as well as his power. At five successive meetings, he laid before his cabinet the whole correspondence, and all the documents, relating to this singular contest; and the cabinet decided unanimously, that the recall of M. Genêt should be immediately demanded of the French government.

Genêt was recalled. In the opinion of America, as well as in his demand upon France, Washington gained a triumph. The federalists indignantly rallied around him. The pretensions and extravagant conduct of Genêt had alienated many persons of the democratic party. Jefferson had not hesitated to support the President against him. A favorable reaction took place, and the contest seemed at an end.

But in government, as well as in war, there are victories which cost dear, and leave the danger still existing. The revolutionary

fever, once more kindled in the United
States, did not depart with a recalled minister. Instead of that harmony of feeling,·
that calm after the storm of passions; instead of that course of prosperity and general moderation, upon which the American
republic was lately congratulating itself,
two parties were there in a hostile attitude,
more widely separated, more violently irritated, than ever. The opposition no longer
confined its attacks to the administration
alone, to the financial measures of government, and to this or that doubtful applica-
tion of legal powers. It had, concealed
within itself, in the democratic associations,
in the periodical press, and among the foreigners who swarmed throughout the
country, a true revolutionary faction, eager
to overturn society and its government, in
order to reconstruct them upon other foundations. "There exists in the United
States," writes Washington to Lafayette,
"a party formed by a combination of
causes, which oppose the government in all
its measures, and are determined, as all
their conduct evinces, by clogging its
wheels, indirectly to change the nature of

it, and to subvert the Constitution. To effect this, no means which have a tendency to accomplish their purposes are left unessayed. The friends of government, who are anxious to maintain its neutrality, and to preserve the country in peace, and adopt measures to secure these objects, are charged by them as being monarchists, aristocrats, and infractors of the Constitution, which, according to their interpretation of it, would be a mere cipher. They arrogated to themselves the sole merit of being the friends of France, when in fact they had no more regard for that nation than for the Grand Turk, further than their own views were promoted by it; denouncing those who differed in opinion, (whose principles are purely American, and whose sole view was to observe a strict neutrality,) as acting under British influence, and being directed by her counsels, or as being her pensioners."* "If the conduct of these men is viewed with indifference; if there are activity and misrepresentation on one side, and supineness on the other, their numbers accumulated by intriguing and

* Washington's Writings, Vol. XI. p. 378.

discontented foreigners under proscription, who were at war with their own governments, and the greater part of them with *all* governments, they will increase, and nothing short of Omniscience can foretell the consequences."*

In the midst of this pressing danger, Jefferson, who was little inclined to engage any further in the contest, and who had announced his intention six months before, and had only delayed putting it in execution at the solicitation of Washington himself, peremptorily withdrew from the cabinet.

The crisis was a formidable one. A general agitation spread throughout the country. The western counties of Pennsylvania resisted with violence the tax on distilled spirits. In Kentucky and Georgia, warlike insurrections, perhaps excited from abroad, threatened, on their own authority, to take forcible possession of Louisiana and Florida, and to engage the nation, in spite of itself, in a conflict with Spain. The war against the Indians continued, always difficult and of doubtful issue. A new Con-

---

* Washington's Writings, Vol. XI. p. 390.

gress had just assembled, full of respect for Washington; but yet the House of Representatives showed itself more reserved in its approbation of his foreign policy, and chose an opposition Speaker by a majority of ten votes. England desired to maintain peace with the United States; but, whether she had doubts of the success of Washington in this system, or acted in obedience to the dictates of her general policy, or from an insolent spirit of contempt, she continued and even aggravated her measures against the commerce of the Americans, whose irritation also increased in its turn. " It has not been the smallest of these embarrassments," writes Washington, "that the domineering spirit of Great Britain should revive again just at this crisis, and the outrageous and insulting conduct of some of her officers should combine therewith to play into the hands of the discontented, and sour the minds of those who are friends to peace. But this, by the bye."*

It was indeed " by the bye," and without any purpose of taking advantage of it in order to weaken his policy or to exalt his

* Washington's Writings, Vol. XI. p. 63.

merit, that he pointed out the obstacles
scattered along his path.   As exempt from
vanity as from indecision, he took pains to
surmount, but not to display them.   At the
time when the ascendency of the democratic party seem to be assured, when the
federalists themselves were wavering, when
severe   measures   proposed in Congress
against England were about, perhaps, to
render war inevitable, Washington suddenly announced to the Senate, by a
message, that he had just nominated one of
the principal leaders of the federal party,
Mr. Jay, Envoy Extraordinary to the Court
of London, in order to attempt to reconcile
the differences between the two nations by
the peaceful instrument of negotiation.

The Senate immediately confirmed his
choice.   The indignation of the opposition
was at its height.   They desired war, and
especially, by means of war, a change of
policy.   The simple continuance of the
present state of affairs promised to lead to
that result.   In so excited a state of feeling,
in the midst of the increasing irritation, a
rumor from Europe, a new insult to the
American flag, the slightest circumstance,

might cause hostilities to break out. Washington, by his sudden resolution, gave a new turn to events. The negotiations might be successful; they made it the duty of the government to await the result. If they failed, he remained in a position to make war himself, and to control it, without his policy's receiving a death-blow.

In order to give to his negotiations the authority of a strong and well-established power, at the same time that he was baffling the hopes of his enemies as to matters abroad, Washington resolved to repress their efforts at home. The resistance of some counties in Pennsylvania to the tax on distilled spirits had become an open rebellion. He announced, by a proclamation, his firm purpose of enforcing the execution of the laws; assembled the militia of Virginia, Maryland, New Jersey, and Pennsylvania itself; formed them into an army; went in person to the places of rendezvous, with a determination to take the command himself if the contest became serious; and did not return to Philadelphia till he had learned, with certainty, that the insurgents would not venture to sustain it. They dis-

10

persed, in point of fact, on the approach of the army, a detachment of which took up winter quarters in the disaffected country.

Washington, on this occasion, felt that stern but deep joy, sometimes granted, in free countries, to a virtuous man who bears firmly the weight of power. Everywhere, especially in the States which were near the scene of the insurrection, good citizens were aware of the danger, and felt their obligation to contribute, by their own efforts, to the support of the laws. The magistrates were resolute, the militia zealous; a strong public opinion silenced the hypocritical sophistries of the advocates of the insurrection; and Washington did his duty with the approbation and support of his country. A moderate compensation, indeed, for the new and bitter trials that awaited him.

At about the same period, his cabinet, which had shared his labors and his glory, withdrew from him. Hamilton, who was the object of a hostility always increasing, after having sustained the contest as long as the success of his plans and his honor required, compelled at length to think of himself and of his family, resigned. Knox followed his example. Thus Washington was surrounded by none but new men, who, though devoted to his course of policy, had much less weight of authority than their predecessors, when Mr. Jay returned from London, bringing the result of those negotiations, the mere announcement of which had excited so much indignation.

The treaty was far from accomplishing all that was to be desired. It did not settle all the questions, nor secure all the interests of the United States; but it put an end to the principal differences of the two nations; it assured the full execution, hitherto delayed by Great Britain, of the agreements entered into with her when she had recognized the independence of the country; it prepared the way for new and more favorable negotiations. In short, it was peace: an assured peace; one which lessened even those evils, which it did not remove.

Washington did not hesitate. He had the rare courage to adhere firmly to a leading principle, and to accept, without a murmur, the imperfections and inconveniences which accompany success. He immediately communicated the treaty to the Senate, who approved it, with the exception of one article, in regard to which a modification was to be required of England. The question still remained in suspense. The opposition made their utmost efforts. Addresses came from Boston, New York, Baltimore, Georgetown, &c., expressing disapprobation of the treaty, and requesting the President not to ratify it. The populace of Philadelphia assembled in a riotous manner, marched through the town, carrying the articles of the treaty at the end of a pole, and formally burned them before the house of the British minister and consul. Washington, who had gone to pass some days at Mount Vernon, returned in haste to Philadelphia, and consulted his cabinet on the question of immediately ratifying the treaty, without awaiting the arrival from London of the modification which even the Senate had declared necessary. This step was a bold one. One member of the cabinet, Randolph, made objections. Washington went on and ratified the treaty. The British government agreed to the modification demanded, and in its turn ratified it.

There still remained the duty of carrying it into effect, which required legislative measures and the intervention of Congress. The contest was renewed in the House of Representatives. Several times the opposition gained a majority. Washington stood firm, in the name of the Constitution, which his opponents also appealed to against him. Finally, at the end of six months, that peace might not be disturbed, in the general conviction that the President would be inflexible, the opposition being rather wearied out than overcome, the measures necessary for carrying the treaty into effect were adopted by a majority of three votes.

Throughout the country, in public meetings and in newspapers, the fury of party exceeded all bounds. From all quarters, every day, addresses full of censure, anonymous letters, invectives, calumnies, threats, were poured out against Washington. Even his integrity was scandalously assailed.

He remained unmoved. He replied to the addresses; " My sense of the treaty has been manifested by its ratification. The principles on which my sanction was given, have been made public. I regret the diversity of opinion. But whatever qualities, manifested in a long and arduous public life, have acquired for me the confidence of my fellow-citizens, let them be assured that they remain unchanged; and that they will continue to be exerted on every occasion, in which the honor, the happiness, and welfare of our common country are immediately involved."*

On the attacks of the press, he said; "I did not believe until lately, that it was within the bounds of probability, hardly within those of possibility, that while I was using my utmost exertions to establish a national character of our own, independent, as far as our obligations and justice would permit, of every nation of the earth; and wished, by steering a steady course, to preserve this country from the horrors of a desolating war, I should be accused of being the enemy of one nation, and subject to the influence of another; and, to prove it, that every act of my administration would be tortured, and the grossest and most insidious misrepresentations of them be made, by giving one side only of a subject, and

* Washington's Writings, Vol. XII. p. 212.

that, too, in such exaggerated and indecent terms as could scarcely be applied to a Nero, a notorious defaulter, or even to a common pickpocket. But enough of this. I have already gone further in the expression of my feelings than I intended."*

Good men, the friends of order and justice, at length perceived that they were leaving their noble champion exposed, without defence, to unworthy attacks. In free countries, falsehood stalks with a bold front; vain would be the attempt to force it to keep concealed; but it is the duty of truth, also, to lift up its head; on these terms alone is liberty a blessing. In their turn, numerous and cordial congratulations, encouraging and grateful addresses, were presented to Washington. And when the close of his second presidency approached, in all parts of the Union, even those where the opposition seemed to prevail, a multitude of voices were raised, to entreat him to accept a third time the highest power which the suffrages of his fellow-citizens could confer.

But his resolution was fixed. He did

* Washington's Writings, Vol. XI. p. 139.

not permit even a discussion of the question. That memorable Farewell Address, in which, as he was returning into the midst of the people whom he had governed, he dispensed to them the last teachings of his long-gathered wisdom, is still, after more than forty years, cherished by them as an object of remembrance, and almost of tenderness of feeling.

"In offering to you, my countrymen, these counsels of an old and affectionate friend, I dare not hope they will make the strong and lasting impression I could wish; that they will control the usual current of the passions, or prevent our nation from running the course, which has hitherto marked the destiny of nations. But, if I may even flatter myself. that they may be productive of some partial benefit, some occasional good; that they may now and then recur to moderate the fury of party spirit, to warn against the mischiefs of foreign intrigue, to guard against the impostures of pretended patriotism; this hope will be a full recompense for the solicitude for your welfare, by which they have been dictated."*   .   .   .   .   .   .

* Washington's Writings, Vol. XII. p. 233.

" Though, in reviewing the incidents of my administration, I am unconscious of intentional error, I am nevertheless too sensible of my defects not to think it probable that I may have committed many errors. Whatever they may be, I fervently beseech the Almighty to avert or mitigate the evils to which they may tend. I shall also carry with me the hope, that my country will never cease to view them with indulgence; and that, after forty-five years of my life dedicated to its service with an upright zeal, the faults of incompetent abilities will be consigned to oblivion, as myself must soon be to the mansions of rest.

" Relying on its kindness in this as in other things, and actuated by that fervent love towards it, which is so natural to a man, who views in it the native soil of himself and his progenitors for several generations; I anticipate with pleasing expectation that retreat, in which I promise myself to realize, without alloy, the sweet enjoyment of partaking, in the midst of my fellow-citizens, the benign influence of good laws under a free government, the ever favorite object of my heart, and the

happy reward, as I trust, of our mutual·
cares, labors, and dangers." *

What an incomparable example of dignity and modesty! How perfect a model
of that respect for the public and for one's
self, which gives to power its moral gran-
deur!

Washington did well to withdraw from
public business. He had entered upon it
at one of those moments, at once difficult
and favorable, when nations, surrounded
by perils, summon all their virtue and all
their wisdom to surmount them. He was
admirably suited to this position. He held
the sentiments and opinions of his age
without slavishness or fanaticism. The
past, its institutions, its interests, its manners, inspired him with neither hatred nor
regret. His thoughts and his ambition did
not impatiently reach forward into the future. The society, in the midst of which
he lived, suited his tastes and his judgment.
He had confidence in its principles and its
destiny ; but a confidence enlightened and
qualified by an accurate instinctive perception of the eternal principles of social order.

* Washington's Writings, Vol. XII. pp. 234, 235.

He served it with heartiness and independence, with that combination of faith and fear which is wisdom in the affairs of the world, as well as before God. On this account, especially, he was qualified to govern it; for democracy requires two things for its tranquillity and its success ; it must feel itself to be trusted and yet restrained, and must believe alike in the genuine devotedness and the moral superiority of its leaders. On these conditions alone can it govern itself while in a process of development, and hope to take a place among the durable and glorious forms of human society. It is the honor of the American people to have, at this period, understood and accepted these conditions. It is the glory of Washington to have been their interpreter and instrument.

He did the two greatest things which, in politics, man can have the privilege of attempting. He maintained, by peace, that independence of his country, which he had acquired by war. He founded a free government, in the name of the principles of order, and by reëstablishing their sway.

When he retired from public life, both

tasks were accomplished, and he could enjoy the result. For, in such high enterprises, the labor which they have cost matters but little. The sweat of any toil is
dried at once on the brow where God
places such laurels.

He retired voluntarily, and a conqueror.
To the very last, his policy had prevailed.
If he had wished, he could still have kept
the direction of it. His successor was one
of his most attached friends, one whom he
had himself designated.

Still the epoch was a critical one. He
had governed successfully for eight years,
a long period in a democratic state, and that
in its infancy. For some time, a policy opposed to his own had been gaining ground.
American society seemed disposed to make
a trial of new paths, more in conformity,
perhaps, with its bias. Perhaps the hour
had come for Washington to quit the arena.
His successor was there overcome. Mr.
Adams was succeeded by Mr. Jefferson,
the leader of the opposition. Since that
time, the democratic party has governed
the United States.

Is this a good or an evil? Could it be

otherwise ? Had the government continued in the hands of the federal party, would it have done better ? Was this possible? What have been the consequences, to the United States, of the triumph of the democratic party ? Have they been carried out to the end, or have they only begun? What changes have the society and constitution of America undergone, what have they yet to undergo, under their influence?

These are great questions; difficult, if I mistake not, for natives to solve, and certainly impossible for a foreigner.

However it may be, one thing is certain; that which Washington did,—the founding of a free government, by order and peace, at the close of the Revolution,—no other policy than his could have accomplished. He has had this true glory; of triumphing, so long as he governed; and of rendering the triumph of his adversaries possible, after him, without disturbance to the state.

More than once, perhaps, this result presented itself to his mind, without disturbing his composure. " With me, a predominant motive has been to endeavor to gain time to our country to settle and mature its yet

recent institutions ; and to progress without
interruption to that degree of strength and
consistency, which is necessary to give it,
humanly speaking, the command of its
own fortunes." *

The people of the United States are vir-
tually the arbiters of their own fortunes.
Washington had aimed at that high object.
He reached his mark.

Who has succeeded like him ? Who has
seen his own success so near and so soon ?
Who has enjoyed, to such a degree and to
the last, the confidence and gratitude of his
country ?

Still, at the close of his life, in the delightful and honorable retirement at Mount
Vernon, which he had so longed for, this
great man, serene as he was, was inwardly
conscious of a slight feeling of lassitude and
melancholy ; a feeling very natural at the
close of a long life employed in the affairs
of men. Power is an oppressive burden ;
and mankind are hard to serve, when one
is struggling virtuously against their passions and their errors. Even success does
not efface the sad impressions which the

* Washington's Writings, Vol. XII. p 234.

contest has given birth to; and the exhaustion, which succeeds the struggle, is still felt in the quiet of repose.

The disposition of the most eminent men, and of the best among the most eminent, to keep aloof from public affairs, in a free democratic society, is a serious fact. Washington, Jefferson, Madison, all ardently sighed for retirement. It would seem as if, in this form of society, the task of government were too severe for men who are capable of comprehending its extent, and desirous of discharging the trust in a proper manner.

Still, to such men alone this task is suited, and ought to be intrusted. Government will be, always and everywhere, the greatest exercise of the faculties of man, and consequently that which requires minds of the highest order. It is for the honor, as well as for the interest, of society, that such minds should be drawn into the administration of its affairs, and retained there; for no institutions, no securities, can supply their place.

And, on the other hand, in men who are worthy of this destiny, all weariness, all sadness of spirit, however it might be permitted in others, is a weakness. Their vocation is labor. Their reward is, indeed, the success of their efforts, but still only in labor. Very often they die, bent under the burden, before the day of recompense arrives. Washington lived to receive it. He deserved and enjoyed both success and repose. Of all great men, he was the most virtuous, and the most fortunate. In this world, God has no higher favors to bestow.

THE END.